All in Good Time

All in Good Time

Don Gutteridge

Originally published by Black Moss Press in 1980.

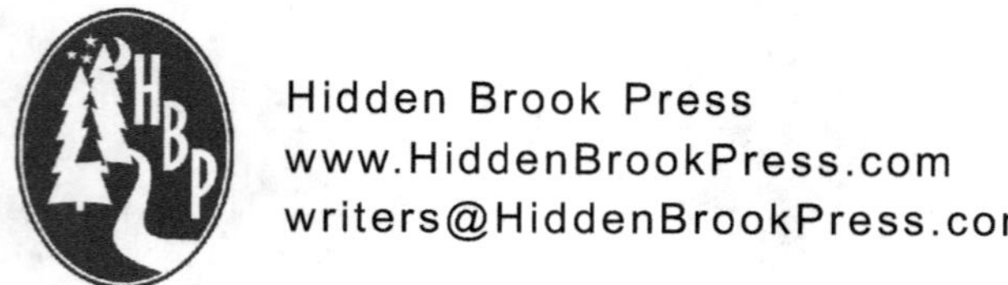

Hidden Brook Press
www.HiddenBrookPress.com
writers@HiddenBrookPress.com

All in Good Time
by Don Gutteridge

Cover Design – Sol Terlson Kennedy
Layout and Design – Richard M. Grove

Typeset in Garamond
Printed and bound in USA
Distributed in USA by Ingram,
        in Canada by Hidden Brook Distribution

Library and Archives Canada Cataloguing in Publication

Title: All in good time / Don Gutteridge.
Names: Gutteridge, Don, 1937 – author.
Description: Originally published: Windsor : Black Moss Press, 1980.
Identifiers: Canadiana (print) 20200153080
        Canadiana (ebook) 20200153099
        ISBN 9781927725955 (softcover)
        ISBN 9781927725962 (EPUB)
        ISBN 9781927725979 (Kindle)
Classification: LCC PS8513.U85 A8 2020
        DDC C813/.54—dc23

For my grandson Tom.

Contents

YPRES
HOOGE
ST ELOI
VIMY RIDGE
BOURLON WOOD

Chapter

1

'IT'S HERE!' Quince was at the window, the curtain eased back discreetly enough to allow her full access to the sidewalk and curb. It didn't occur to her that she was allowing her neighbours full access to her own right eye, right cheek and most of her sharp little nose.

'What's here,' snapped the Reeve from the bedroom doorway.

'A Packard, I think,' she said, letting the curtain drift naturally back into place.

'What year?' he said. He was having the customary skirmish with his tie.

'Black,' said Quince, the wind having conveniently started up again. 'And he's got a uniform, gray, with some kinda yellow — he's getting out!'

The Reeve, his mind on more significant matters, did not hear this last remark. Goddam tie! He fought it with managed fury, more of a mental fight than a physical one: his imagination racing as it often did far ahead of his actions, his puzzled fingers.

The Chauffeur had indeed gotten out of the black Packard, its motor still running, giving out, every once in a while, self-important puffs of exhaust which the below-zero village air seized and held.

But in spite of the absolute stillness of the cold, a wind did seem to be blowing down Wellington Street, east to west, with particular intent on a number of the town's front-room curtains.

Quince gave up all pretense and just stared. He was so tall! His uniform looked as if it had been steam-pressed after he'd put it on! Of course, he was dark-complexioned and just vaguely, enticingly, foreign. Despite his size and importance, he came up the frozen walk without the least scrunching sound; his footprints were a flawless signature on the day's dust of snow.

The Reeve had accepted the 'draw' with as much good grace as he could muster on a day as important as this. The tie's thoughts went unrecorded as he was now waving at the elusive sleeve of his overcoat. Christ! he was going to sweat. He hated that; it was worse than a tie with battle-experience, or the bits of toilet paper he was always forgetting to remove from the morning's razor-cut. He'd start to ooze before he went out, and then the uncompromising overcoat would hold it in, steamy and accumulating, so when he finally got the damn thing off, shivering and clammy, the new tweed suit would look as if he had just come through a quick but vindictive cloud-burst.

Now the left galosh was at it! Half in, half out. On a good day you just gave it a curse and a stomp and it popped into place.

It wasn't a good day.

Quince was making little noises that might have been words, but the Reeve had no time for breaking codes — not this evening anyway. She seemed to be gesturing towards the door. Why was she so gauche at times like this? These moments which, observed from the less hectic perspective of a future time, would seem as turning points in their lives. He loved her, though, in spite of it, and that thought flicked magnanimously through his mind as he wrapped the new white silk scarf about his neck and forced the last button of his coat to concede. Yes, she was a country-girl, but there were virtues nonetheless — they would see that someday, and judge that he had chosen wisely.

But it was annoying (the scarf failed to find its own level, one fluffy end leaking out)—aggravating that she would think the Mayor's chauffeur would pull up to the house, get out and traipse up the walk to fetch him like a common person — no, he'd seen it done on the newsreels enough to realize that chauffeurs arrived on time and merely waited, the vip materializing miraculously from his hotel or office or parliamentary mansion, the chauffeur, without a sideways glance, out and around the limousine, door held rigid just in time — like the whole thing was scripted and rehearsed: without a hitch. It was downright aggravating that she should race him to the door, fling it open and embarrass them both.

'For Christ sakes, halt, woman!'

Quince froze.

With a cinematic gesture the Reeve flung open his front door (the film running perfectly before him, he felt his body fit its demands as if it had been bom to the manner). Here was no time to notice or care about a gimpy left golash or a white scarf trickling inch by inch into the snow.

* * *

'ARE YOU all right, sir?'

He wasn't, but what do you say sitting half-dazed in your own snowbank?

The Chauffeur, being a large man and keeping both eyes open, had been able to step partly aside when the Reeve, tangled

3

in the treacherous scarf, had come headlong and somewhat oblong towards him.

Never had his European breeding been so necessary.

* * *

WHEN EVERY SPECK of snow had been brushed off him, twice, and the scarf tied securely in a double-hitch, the Reeve's composure began to return. In fact he thought that in retrospect he might come to see the virtue of this ill-luck, knowing they were all watching him with either their left or right eye — and seeing not merely the pratfall but its after- math: this solicitous, painfully deferential brushing-down he was being given in front of them all.

'Reeve Macintosh?'

'Yes.'

'May we go now, sir?'

'Yes, my good man. And thank you. The wife's always had trouble doing up that scarf proper. Should do these things ourselves, shouldn't we?'

For a second the Mayor's chauffeur looked startled — abashed — as if his continental breeding were not up to it.

'Didn't mean that quite the way it sounded,' the Reeve

chuckled noisily, wondering why the man didn't move to open the door of the patient black Packard. 'But you know women, eh?'

The man didn't move. What he thought of women he kept to himself, but he did clear his throat heavily, making a sort of nod and a wink with his right eye.

'Got something in your eye?' the Reeve said, wondering how he was going to nudge this guy towards the Packard.

'Ah, sir, uh, your...' Blink. Blink again.

'Shall we go, my good man?'

Did the poor bugger have an incurable twitch? St. Vitus' Dance? How could he drive with one eye going twitch-twitch all the time?

'Uh, on your chin, sir.'

'Ohhhh.' Then: 'Thank you, my good man.'

In the snow by the walk who would have noticed a miniature white and red toilet-paper flag tossed without ceremony from the Reeve's chin?

* * *

AS THE LIMOUSINE and its Chauffeur and its very important person moved down Michigan Ave towards the City, in every window where the random wind had blown that hour could be seen a single, steamy breath-mark: from north to south a sentence of perfect 'ohs'.

* * *

THEY WERE JUST CROSSING the tracks that separated the Point from the City, divided reeve-ship from mayordom and even headier destinies — and the Reeve felt the flush of blood in his cheeks, the extra heartbeat. He hoped the Mayor's chauffeur had not noticed, for he might assume that the Air-Temp control was too high or something, when it was really quite perfect. Really. The snow all down the front of his coat (some had gone too deeply in to be brushed off) had not only melted very nicely, it had begun to dry out with what he thought was decent convenience. But whenever he moved from his own village to the City that utterly surrounded it from Bay to Lake (a necklace or a noose depending upon your political blush) — he could not, dammit he would not, suppress this feeling of expansiveness, of unsanctioned joy, of downright generosity. (He might had said 'magnanimity' but after having Quince check it out in the Concise Oxford, he had stumbled in pronouncing it in front of the Lodge brothers, and then when he did get it right later in the speech, the looks of dismay on the faces of the brethren were even more unsettling — he had decided then and there that one could only do so much as Reeve of a village with no hope of expansion unless one counted houseboats or ice-fishing tents.)

No, he would not suppress it, nor would he deny to the world that part of it was generated by pride — well-earned, mind you, and always religiously in check — but a healthy expansionary pride, the kind that had built this very City, the heart's core of those visionaries who dreamed of its great arc swinging from Bay to Lake, and to hell with the Point, the insignificant villages which have always stood in the way of historical progress, the Necessity of the times ...

'Pardon, sir?'

'Eh?'

'You were addressing me, sir?'

Mumbling again. Gotta watch that. Yet what could be done about it? The mind racing with words — he thought sometimes his head would burst like a baked apple with the sheer tension of its unarticulated sentences.

'I was saying it's a very cold evening. My good man.'

'Yes, sir.'

'You've got as much snow here as we have in the Point.'

'Indeed, sir.'

They were so passionless, these servants of the powerful. He admired them. Must be bred into them ... like politicians. Yes, they were — if one dare not stretch the analogy too far — quite a bit the same: the politician must control his feelings at every instance, channel them calculatingly (as he himself had in numerous bids for high office), but always of course directed towards the public good. And the servant: with his discipline, his dedication to the master, was indeed part of the whole chain of command, the predestined scheme of things. Who else kept these snow-enclosed mansions here along the Lambton Road so sedate, so dignified, so worthy of the veneration of the common folk? And all the while running those households within with such restrained efficiency, with the competence of those bred and ordained to aid the rule of others over us. Yes, yes, he was onto something here. If only Quince had remembered to put his note-pad in his tweed- jacket (she hadn't). He must get this down; try it out on the Mayor. That was it! A grand analogy with visionary sweep, for there was now — as he thought about it so very close to these palaces of the powerful along Lambton Road — there was no doubt as to why he had been so peremptorily summoned. Two civic leaders greeting one another, a discreet smile, the acknowledgement made — without words; the Reeve's time had indeed come. 'Ontario is ripe for a Macintosh,' he would jest a little indiscreetly, later over confidential brandies, and the Mayor would laugh, trying without success to disguise his envy of such a ready wit. But what could he say? It was time.

And damn cold! The wind shot up his half-dried pantlegs and popped him a double-jab on the testicles.

'Christ, man, close the window!' He tried to keep the petulance out of his voice, leaning forward with a decisive shoulder to get the Chauffeur's attention.

He wasn't there! Fled? A plot?

'We're here, sir.' Very loud.

The chill air bit at the well-bred servant standing with the rear door rigid.

'Ah, yes, patience, my good man. I was just fixing some papers here in my … briefcase.' No briefcase. On the bedroom table near Quince's vanishing cream. Was there no one to serve?

'The Mayor is waiting, sir.' The icy downdraft seemed to have sketched on the man's face the faintest arc of a smile.

Well, if he'd had time and hadn't stumbled over the Chauffeur's inadvertent left boot, the Reeve would soon have wiped that smirk off. Instead, he made his most — magnanimous — gesture towards the stern verandah straight ahead of him.

* * *

'YOU MUSTN'T ASSUME, my good fellow, that we haven't been keeping our eye on you down there in the village. I know, I know we up here in the City must appear to be, ah, aloof at times, but I assure you …'

When William Dougall MacAdorey pronounced the word 'aloof', one listened, mesmerized by the Scottish burr (only slightly affected after four generations), but more by the unreleased power one knew lay coiled in the very casualness with which it slid off the tongue. And the Reeve was listening, here in the Library (that's what he would have to call his comer of the new rumpus-room, though it took Quince positively years to get used to new names for things; for example, she still called it the 'front room' despite his insistence on 'living room' when the Postmaster and Fire Chief dropped in); and here in the early hours of the coldest night of the year, with a scrupulously cozy fire before them, the accommodating leather chairs stuck right through to their buttocks, with three or four brandies and two Cuban cigars adrift behind them — unimportant preludes to the man-talk, the buzz of power embellishing the room.

'No, not at all ... your career has been monitored from its inception — another brandy? Why, of course. Not the best, I'm afraid. Bloody Krauts have drunk up all the Courvoisier.' French accent. Long sigh. 'But War or no War, as you well know, politics must go on. How else would the world run?'

Indeed, how else? What a turn of phrase the Mayor had. The Reeve sipped his fourth brandy a little more defensively this time, and this time cupping both his hands round the odd-shaped goblet, and letting his nose steal over the rim.

'True, but when it's over we don't want those boys who are spilling their blood, their Christian blood, over there for us, mind you, we don't want them coming back here and finding out we haven't been doing our share. No sir, this city has got to grow, and when we've finished up this little skirmish — oh, sorry. Caught cold?'

The Reeve's sneeze blew not only the noxious brandy fumes out of harm's way but most of the gray, delicately- formed corpses of Cuban cigar-ash as well.

'Yes, sir, I believe I may have. Colder here than in the Highlands, eh?' He'd managed that quip quite dextrously, and the Mayor was good enough to gaze into his ersatz, flame-lit brandy while the Reeve brushed the ash off his best tweed suit.

'And so we have been making plans, as I have said, and they require for their fulfilment men of your calibre, who've been through the political wars.'

The fumes were in his head now, a cozy little fireplace of

them, making his insides as warm and comfortable and winter-vulnerable as his flesh, here in the Library of William Dougall MacAdorey, whose own political wars had been Armageddons compared with his own: City Councillor, Chairman of the School Board, mla for two terms before acceding to the call from Parliament, which he selflessly answered (after one rude and unforgiveable setback), carrying the City's hopes, and the Point's as well, to the country's nerve-centre for four self-sacrificing years. After which one would have thought this man of family and breeding would have retired to his newly-constructed homestead here on the historic Lambton Road (built by his newly-formed construction company, which even now was so busy with war contracts the man had scarcely time to enjoy his second-best brandy). One would have assumed graceful retirement to the Sabine farm (he was raising beef in the township for the cause) — but no, this doughty Scots, whose forebears had dreamed the first grist-mill not more than five miles from where they sat, cozy and safe in a below-zero world, this man had taken on without complaint the dual burdens of the Mayorality and the presidency of the local branch of the Party itself.

'Eight straight wins, no defeats. Even I didn't manage that, my dear fellow.'

Oh that self-deprecating chuckle! What magna — what generosity!

'Certainly, sir, by all means. Take the box of them if you like. At least Cuba's on our side, eh'

The wit again. Unforced, inclusive. Sealing confidences like the smoke of the Indian's peace-pipes in the log-warm teepee ... yes, that was the feeling, the caress of this velvet smoke in his throat, the liquor magnifying every word and nuance flowing between them. Yes, he was talking now, he could distinguish clearly his own voice, carrying forth its own cause, waiting for the just moment, the inevitable request each knew would be made, but only when the ceremony was complete, the proper gods appeased.

'Yes, yes,' he heard himself say, agreeing without hesitation to such evident perspicacity. 'That's precisely my way of seeing it.'

Smoke rose, curled, drifted as if trying to make signs of some sort, tiny puff-words, but so thin, so —

'So you do begin to see the drift of this, my dear Macintosh. What we need is leadership in this cause — and it's a just cause as you know — a man who's proven he's got his constituents in his hip-pocket, so to speak. After all, ah, incorporation is a large step ...'

'Yes, yes, I completely agree with your Worship.' Though he wished his Worship would go over that 'cause' just a bit more clearly; but then they were, after all's said and done, members of the same Party.

His brandy glass seemed to have filled itself again. He sipped one-handed.

'I can't impress upon you too much, Macintosh ol' fellow, just how badly we need experienced men. Why, old Menzies is barely hanging on, you know.' Voice lowered, leaning in through the brandy haze. 'And only because of the Coalition Cabinet, you understand. Health's bad. Yes, really bad — even his wife doesn't know.'

'Yes, yes. Precisely.'

'Brave old soldier, though. Naturally I feel particularly safe in telling you this because it's now Party business, you see, and with the old boy's liver about to do a swan-dive, so to speak, we'll naturally be in the market for a candidate soon as this Trouble's over with, and ...'

Yes, yes, I see.

Two old chieftains (well, one not so old) in the conspiratorial wigwam, letting the smoke-dreams make words for them, a setting for the ceremonial act which would conclude with the seal of their grand x's on this treaty, this testament. H.R. Macintosh, mp for Huron Lake — well, there'd be no forgetting his roots, the friends who'd helped him on his way up.

'... just how, ah, thorny an issue it is at this time. Without your help it simply won't come off. But as I've hinted, Horace, in the strict secrecy of this room, the rewards could be high, could reach far beyond this local issue of — shall we call it 'consolidation'? One must get the right phrase in politics, mustn't one? What do you think, Horace, from the local perspective?'

Yes, yes, I see. I agree completely. Yes, yes, a penetrating, yes, penetrating ...

'Go ahead, it's Bill from now on, old fellow.'

Yes, yes, I agree completely.

As sitting member he would be able to put the Point on the map, people would know where it was, the villagers would no longer have to say to strangers they were from the City to avoid embarrassment, the Point would be a dateline in The Star, he would be quoted verbatim ...

'You see we've got to consolidate, it's not merely a question of administrative efficiency, and God knows after the War we'll need ...'

The books on all three walls had separate titles; he hadn't noticed till now. When he first came in they were like a fancy leather wallpaper. Was it possible that the Mayor, his Worship,

Bill, had read them all? Knew all the words and ideas? Yes, I see. You needed the sentences, there was no doubt about that: he himself had recognized that truth speaking to the Lodge or at the Council meetings over the Fire Hall; but where did you get them from? Of course, precisely.

'... complete and unrestrained access to the shoreline from

the Bay to the Lake; consolidated schools, a single council to serve the general interest. By God, Horace, this country's going to start booming when all the Fuss is over.'

Yes, yes. And I want to be there. Do you understand my point, sir?

'You're perfectly right; we know it won't be easy; you guys down there have been putting up a pretty gutsy fight over the issue, and I like that, Horace, I do. But remember that this sort of, ah, 'joint-effort' is progress, and we need a guy with your record, your gutsiness, so to speak, to deliver the vote, it's as plain as that. And then there's the long look into the future, as I've said in the strictest candour. Old Menzies just can't keep the nozzle out of his mouth ...'

God, when he got home he would fill his cupboards with this brandy, second-best or not; it made it all so vivid, words he would never have been able to fathom were clarified here in the trembling brandy-warmth, the log-coziness — that Scot's voice burred with authority, its sentences like rich pedigrees of persuasion.

Who would not answer?

'Ah, very good. That's what I knew you'd say, Horace. Very good indeed.'

Hand on his arm.

'Let me help you. Damn fire's too hot in here; makes a fellow dizzy, eh?'

A hand on each arm now. Breathing in both ears. Walking.

Liquor fizzing in the brain. Murky corridor.

'Good idea. Emily and I'll have you and the good woman down for tea real soon. Meantime I'll set up the meetings as you suggested, Horace.'

The cold. Right through his coat. Interrogative. An icy question mark on each of his apple-red cheeks.

'Watch your step, sir.'

* * *

QUINCE HAD LET the furnace go out. For Christ sakes, the room is like a tomb. No wonder. With a shudder he realized he was stark naked, his clothes a defeated heap on the floor beside the dresser. No pajamas.

She was sleeping, her breath coming in and out: white puffs in the dark room, regular and contented. Well, he had things to say, and they could not wait for morning or a full furnace or a night's sleep. The world had moved while the village slept.

He nudged her. The puffs kept puffing. He shook her, letting his own shivering nakedness jerk at her flesh.

'Ohhhh ... mmmmm.'

Puff, puff.

He ripped the covers right off the bed, and in so doing dragged Quince's floppy nightgown halfway up her back. She jumped awake, straight up, exposing a blush on two perfectly-shaped little apple-buttocks, then, swivelling around, faced the intruder.

'Oh, Horace, it's you! You — '

'Darling, I've had such a — '

'Your pajamas!?'

' — wonderful evening. You wouldn't believe — '

'The fire's out! It's like a dungeon in here!'

' — that house, you really wouldn't believe it.'

'You said you'd bank it before you — where's your pajamas?'
'Oh Quince, Quince, I've such things to tell you.'

'But Horace, your pajamas, the fire's — '

'I've such things ... such ... such — '

The Reeve of all the village collapsed oblong beside Quince, stunned in mid-word as if the sentence-machine inside his head had miraculously shut itself off at the same instant as his arms aimed slowly out and around the presence of his wife's flesh still warm from its easy sleep. She saw his meaning at once. Without words.

'Yes, darling. Let me pull up the eiderdown.'

For the moment they spoke the only language they knew.

* * *

BUT BACK THERE in the snow-bound City, what words had passed his lips? What commitment given? What, in God's name, had he said yes to?

Yes or not, the morning waited, with a cold furnace.

* * *

SOMETIME BEFORE THE SUN rose he remembered saying 'I love you, Quince.'

1945
Chapter

2

THE REEVE WAS BIDING his time, like everyone else
marooned by the War on this forlorn peninsula, waiting for life
to revive, and in particular the political life. Oh he had been
returned to the Reeveship without difficulty in forty-one and
forty-three — his three successive terms rivalling those of the
legendary Cap Dowling back in the 1880's, after the incorporation of the village, at the dawn of time, so to speak. Of
course, in them days the railroads ran the town and ol' Cap was,
quite simply, their man. Whereas he had done it on his own; the
last time by acclamation. Imagine that. All good fortune it
seemed having flowed in an underailable line from a single event
— a midnight tête-à-tête with William Dougall MacAdorey.
There is a tide in the affairs of —

'Good evening, Reeve.'

Ah, young Mrs. Roberts, the former lovely Miss Purdy.

'And a good evening it is,' replied the Reeve with only a
touch of condescension as he stooped automatically over the
baby-basket on the yellow sled and planted a practised kiss on
the blanketed child. (Babies to kiss were getting harder to find.)

'And a darling baby you have — '

'Groceries,' said the former Miss Purdy, abashed. 'For my
mother.'

16

'And how's her lumbago?' said the Reeve barely missing a beat.

It was a clear mid-winter evening. The air was sharp, so you could feel your own breathing, in and out, cold then warm, the blood rising deliberately to test it. Overhead the stars stretched from rim to rim, a whole village captive in their radiant grip.

That business of the Party's nomination had had to be put off. He understood perfectly. With the War dragging on so long, and so much fiercer than anybody imagined, naturally they could not go with a radical candidate. Old Menzies, puffed liver and all, would have to do till the smoke cleared a little. Still, MacAdorey had retired to take care of his burdensome business interests, retaining only the regional presidency of the provincial wing of the Party; there was always a provincial seat. And annexation? (He must remember to say consolidation.) Inevitable; though the War was making words like inevitable less comforting than they used to be. Nevertheless, the cause was all: the world itself was in danger of annexation; how could one even think of discussing the City's inalienable right to incorporate the Point, to nudge its prosperity to the geographical limit. The Reeve was a patriot. No one had ever questioned him on that score. And to his credit, he had never, since that fateful meeting, even asked that promises made before the grim fact of war be kept. He knew the value of loyalty; of patience; and silence.

'Going to the meeting, Red?'

'Why, ah, certainly, Mr. Reeve,' said the grocer with a slight skidding on the soft 'c' as he passed the Reeve. 'Just finishing my deliveries,' he explained, stopping and turning uncertainly. 'Can't get away from some of these old women, you know. Takes all day to deliver half a dozen boxes.'

'It's the War,' said the Reeve helpfully.

'No husbands around for them to yak to or nag at. Talk the ear off a corn-shock.'

The Reeve nodded. 'Bringing the missus along?'

Some tiny beam of recollection flickered between the inflamed cheeks. 'She wouldn't miss it. Just left Wee Bessie at the store. Going home to get her.'

Wee Bessie was a truck not a wife, though the two occasionally became confused.

'That way,' said the Reeve, turning him north. He liked to be helpful.

But the tide had turned. The War was being won on those far beaches, not unlike their own, he surmised. In swamps like those below the Bridge, and forests twenty times as big as First Bush which kept the City from touching the eastern edge of the village. Was being won with the courage of village boys, some of whose names would be chiselled on the Monument in the centre of town after it was, finally, over. 'Over by spring,' The Reporter was saying twice a week. He was a patriot, no one to deny that, but he had been silent long enough. The people needed leadership; the War had been going on so long that they were getting used to it, thinking out of habit that life was like this or that, and would somehow carry on in the same way even when the boys came back. Reeve Macintosh knew differently. He was a politician by instinct and by lifelong training — a political animal (or fruit, as he sometimes remarked on the platform making a small joke against himself). Change would be upon them. Time would rev up again, and they must all move with the times. And so it was he, their acclaimed leader who had called the meeting for this night. Friday, seven o'clock at the Lodge Hall beside the Monument in the centre of town.

'Going to the meeting?' he said to Martha Gibson who was coming towards him on the other side of Michigan Ave, head down, slouched against the windless cold, her lower body hidden by the drifts from the recent blizzard.

She didn't reply, turning instead onto Princess Street, clutching her cloth coat with both arms and staring at the narrow path through the snow as if it were the only certainty in an unravelling universe.

'Missing in action,' the Reeve remembered aloud, thinking of Guy Gibson's youthful smile, that booming voice full of hope and scorn echoing across the Rink below the Bridge when there were real hockey games in the Point, and real players with promise, when winning and losing seemed to bear significance beyond the game. They carried on, of course; they had to. The old traditions — robbed of their central, life-espousing power by the consuming ritual of battle — had to be maintained at all costs: marriage, birth, love, ordinary death, the pranks of fatherless children, the necessary games. Even politics.

The moon had almost reached its full hour: a silver shield just above the horizon, hanging like a newly-minted nickel just below the span of the Bridge that linked two nations. Its white sheen, though borrowed, seemed destined this February evening of 1945 for the village alone, and married to the incandescent snow which had poured down upon them days before like a perfect camouflage. But tonight moon and stars were cousin, giving freely of light the hospitable snow returned tenfold. The Reeve could survey his holdings.

And what he couldn't see, he could hear. Down in the swamps behind the Lodge he could hear the boys playing shinney in the moonlight: the crack of sticks like erratic gunfire, the muffled collision of blade and snowy ice, the tender curses of the second-best, too-young warriors. The Underhill boys would be there, and Skinny McKeough; their brothers, who once carried the village banner to the ends of the province, were far away. In their absence these schoolboys would make do, and he for one had cheered them as lustily as he had the brilliant Bill Underhill bound for the Big League before the War diminished all heroes.

The meeting tonight would change all that. The War was being won; preparations must be made. The Reeve had sought no advice, asked no approval. The Party had made him a promise and a commitment. Five years had slipped by in mutual silence, and he, the Reeve of the people, had made his own decision. Not even Quince knew what he was about to announce. (He promised himself he would not think in that direction tonight.)

When he had called on MacAdorey to break the news, to make the audacious offer, he had been met with stunned silence (even longtime Party commanders could be silenced by daring). MacAdorey no doubt wondered how he had known that the new Governor-General was due to visit the area, but he had his sources and they would remain as secret as the seed in the heart of the first Macintosh. But frontal assault will out every time, and so it had on this occasion. A straight tit-for-tat deal, the Reeve had said, frontally. Yes, the commandant had smiled, disguising his anxiety, a quid-pro-quo (he must remember to use that in his speech): the Governor- General for Annexation. They shook hands on it, MacAdorey's citified gesture crushed in the grip of a man seasoned not only by local politics but by the honest labour of snow-removal and garbage collection. He did not tell MacAdorey of his play to include the hockey game in the festivities; let him read it in the papers! And marvel.

'Good evening, Mr. Hornby.'

The new church organist almost bumped into him, but the Reeve stepped nimbly aside.

'Oh, good evening, Horace.'

The Reeve winced. 'Going to the meeting?' he asked, pulling his left leg out of the snowbank.

'Nice job you did on the roads,' said Cameron Hornby, giving the Reeve a hand with his left galosh.

'That's what they pay me for. Don't start for an hour yet. I'm just going down early to get things in order.'

'Ah yes, I heard about it. I'll try to be there if I can. I've got some new music to go over, for Sunday, you see. Being new and all.'

'I understand perfectly, young man. Perfectly.'

Cam Hornby, young and far too handsome for a church organist, nodded, walked on and turned not towards the Church but down Princess Street.

'Probably votes Grit,' muttered the Reeve.

Nothing, not even his twisted left galosh, could disturb his equanimity on this evening of evenings. Even the announcement of the meeting had been big time: a handwritten, hectographed letter over his personal signature placed in every mailbox at the Post Office, with a dozen more for general delivery, just in case. And no details. Merely the Reeve calling a meeting of all of the people to make two important announcements that would affect the lives of every man, woman and child in the Point. 'The War's over?' Mitch Strong the Postmaster had speculated. 'Almost,' the Reeve rejoined with a wink. Let them wonder and be amazed. He would pronounce, and harvest approval. No one could possible object —

The object that struck the Reeve was definitely a snowball, one that had resided in its maker's fist for some considerable time. Fortunately, it caught the target flush on its bulbous nose, otherwise it might have blackened an eye. And since the Reeve's nose was customarily red, only the internal swelling would offer any impediment to his performance — these were his thoughts as he tumbled sideways into the snowbank he himself had made with the municipal plough the previous day.

'Jesus Christ!'

'The Reeve swore! The Reeve swore!'

'Bugger off, you little buggers!' spouted the Reeve, too busy with scrambling for his dignity to be aware of any redundancy.

'Your grandmother washes in pigeon-shit!' yelled the largest little bugger.

'Green pigeon-shit!' mimicked his smaller accomplice before they both disappeared towards the snow-draped Monument by the Lodge Hall.

No respect. No respect at all. He knew who they were, all right. Martha Gibson's boy (green pigeon-shit) and Orie Wollochuk, one of the Polack kids from Pott's Lane. Ah, well, be charitable; there's a war on. Little Guy had been only four or so when his Dad left for Europe. Fatherless. And a mother too numbed by worry, and now grief, to be both mother and father to the boy. Wollochuk was another case altogether — one of the dozen or so runny-nosed ragamuffins let loose on the town from their collection of shanties near the cn tracks. Foreigners, all of them, leeches on the body politic. And micks to boot, voting Grit if they ever bothered to vote at all. And Marovitch, the bootlegger, feeding them all with the devil's dream-drink. He'd have to speak to Chief Piersall, soon, about a raid. After the festivities, of course. No use stirring up discord beforehand.

'Ouch!' He turned to make sure no one had heard, then touched his flaming nose with more care this time. Damn that Polack brat! How was he to get any resonance in his delivery? In the most important political speech of is life, on this, the most important night in the almost-hundred-year history of the village.

No one heard or saw. They were all finishing up their suppers, getting ready to stroll the few short blocks to the Lodge Hall for the seven o'clock gathering. He stepped briskly now, regaining his form, collecting his thoughts for the effort to come. Not even notes. He would jettison his note-card and speak ex tempore like the orators of old. It suited his style, his composed confidence.

Besides the pain in the interior of his nose, only one other burr stuck on his backside, so to speak. Quince. He had sworn a vow not to think on it any more. And he didn't; at least not in the daylight. But at night, lying beside her withering flesh, listening to her pretend-sleep, he could not help it. If he had stopped loving her, it would be easier to explain it all, but in a strange way he had not. The outward courtesies were strictly observed — a peck on the cheek before he braved the blizzards in the bright red municipal truck; her puckered lips warm on his frozen cheek in the evening; the farm-size suppers kept hot in the patient oven. Her sympathy, unending it seemed, as he talked out his dreams night after night, year after year, towards the future that always eluded him, in the house he had built for her on Wellington Street right after the Great War in the bloom of their flawless union. And their harboured lust — cloaked by the condoning dark, released mutually, held for the moment, never talked of in daylight: that part had been so good. All along he had accepted at face value her unspoken assurance of his grand plans — youngest councillor in the Point's long history, faithful worker for the Party, then the Reeve-ship, the powers-that-be in Toronto sitting up in their club-rooms to take notice of a rising star at the western edge of the vast province. All along she had been at his side (not literally because she was too shy to mount the public stage) in spirit, her hopes ascending with his. The good wife: keeping the hearth stoked and a warm pallet for the fatigued chieftain. So he had thought. And had reason to believe.

But then in sight of their goal, at the moment when both of them would be launched out of this backwoods' rink, so to speak, onto the world's rostrum, it ended. The daily courtesies continued, of course, in their fixed rhythms, so reassuring in their meticulous repetition that neither participant recognized at first the love they symbolized and cemented had ceased to be. The Reeve knew now. He knew because the power that sustained it — the nightly surrender and possession — had withered and fallen away. Oh, he still talked out his dreams right up to the end, but when the weeks went by and too many nights were spent back-to-back, he knew she was not sharing them. She had made a home for him; that was now clear. And looking back on it with the clarity of hindsight, he saw that it had never been possible. She was a country girl; she would have been awkward, ungainly, beside him on the political stage. He should have known that from the beginning. He shuddered now to think of the embarrassment, the downright shame he would have endured — Quince at a cocktail party! Making small-talk with Mr. MacAdorey, or the Premier himself! Good Lord, she still said 'ain't' and 'he don't'!

How could he not have seen this before? Had she been listening to his heart's hope all these years and thinking only of his being a Reeve? A Reeve who drove the village truck to make his way in this cruel world? The unfairness of it all struck him with dreadful irony, but he struggled valiantly against self-pity. He couldn't stand it in others and would not allow himself to even contemplate it. It was unworthy of a man headed for high office, for a life of service to his fellow man.

The appearance of Gloria Sawbush in his life had been a

result of his clairvoyance, not a cause. On that score his conscience was clear. Quince was growing old while he, rejuvenated by his gathering powers, felt younger at forty- seven than he had at twenty. Their pale bodies clinging to the dark no longer found the mutual and sustaining satisfaction. More and more she had feigned sleep when he, exhausted from a long day on the garbage truck (he drove and gave orders) and tortured hours at his desk poring over Party business (elections were won in the polling districts not the backrooms), crawled into bed hungry for solace and relief. Sometimes after he had with difficulty fallen into the first deep sleep, she would rouse herself, turn to him and press her pathetic breasts to his back, but he knew there was no heart in it and did not deign to acknowledge the gesture.

Little wonder, then, that Gloria Sawbush presented herself uniquely to him. Perhaps it could be admitted that some justice resided in this world after all. Gloria Sawbush: a genuine City girl, motherless and come to stay with her aunts, the Misses Robertson, while her father was off to Ottawa working for the cause in some big government commission. Twenty-three, with cheeks as pink as peonies, eyes like agate, hair as yellow as cut straw, and a genuine certificate of Senior Matriculation from the Collegiate Institute. Certainly, it was not mere chance that brought her application for recording secretary of the village Council to his attention. Sure, he'd endured a lot of spiteful talk when he had preferred her over Maggie Stoneham, the retired schoolteacher, but after all is said and done she could not take shorthand. Gloria could. She was also, like her father, an active supporter of the Party. Let them talk. They would all be humming a different tune after the hoedown tonight!

'What's that you said, Reeve?'

'Uh?'

'I said what were you saying? Sounded like you was muttering away to yourself.'

'I was asking how you've been lately? Haven't seen you for a coon's age.'

'Touch of the grippe,' said Maxie Wise, still staring curiously at the Reeve. Maxie, Secretary-Treasurer of the Council and Chairman-designate for the special meeting, had come down early to open up the Hall.

'You've been standing in front of the Monument for five minutes,' Maxie said. 'You okay?'

'Yes, I'm fine. Getting the tongue loosened for the big speech.'

'Mighty mysterious you are about this business. Guess just about everybody'll be here.'

'Yes, yes.'

The Reeve was indeed standing directly in front of the Monument, erected by the village fathers after the Great War. It was a simple pillar set upon a double pedestal, the scroll of the village-dead engraved against time along its four sides. On top and overlooking the whole town were the shoulders and helmeted head of the unknown soldier, his eyes in the cement seemingly blank; or merely closed, dreaming his own darkly private, inexpiable thoughts.

The name directly in front of the Reeve, at eye level, visible to him and the searching glance of Maxie Wise, was that of his twin brother:

EDGAR GEORGE MACINTOSH
Killed in Action
Ypres, 1916

Chapter

3

SHE WAS GETTING READY for her music lesson at seven. Music lessons, in the middle of the War. It was likely that both pupil and teacher knew the meaning of the music so far, and probably the whole town. Martha did not care; let them think whatever their small minds could burrow into. But, of course, she did. At moments like these with the house deathly quiet and its silence like a sounding-board for her own wayward thoughts, she was smothered by fear and guilt. At the same time a barely repressed rage rose in her, one she had never felt before: an anger without a name.

Damn! The plate lay in several pieces on the linoleum beside the sink, and she saw with regret that it was Little Guy's plate, the one his father had given him just before leaving. Little Guy barely remembered his Dad and she in her wicked reverie had just destroyed one of the few links that kept their lives connected. Oh well, it served her right. There's no such thing as an accident, her mother always said. She was right. If so, then what was the meaning of the act that propelled the telegram thousands of miles over sea and land and out of the worst blizzard of the village-winter? Missing in Action. Her life, their life, disconnected, and what God could convince her that it was not a random selection? Otherwise what reason could He offer,

27

even in the long view from His height? There are no accidents.

At first: shock, a disabling numbness that six weeks had not diminished. The neighbours, having seen the cab like a hearse through the snow, waited just an hour before they came over. Out of respect. For what?

'Mine came in the middle of the night,' said Mrs. Taylor, a youthful fifty-two and almost thirty years a practising widow. 'We'd only been married a month before his call-up. I'll never forget it saying "missing in action" and me thinking "oh, thank God, at least he's not dead" and then the awful shock when my friends, they were widows themselves poor dears, they tried to tell me in the nicest possible way not to even think my darling Harold was alive, only one in a million was ever found alive in that awful place, and I recollect how I struggled not to believe that, oh I wanted so much to keep that little bit of hope alive, 'cause it was like having just a little bit of dear Harold left, but then the second telegram come, just as they said it would, only three days later, and I was a widow. Only one month Mrs. Gibson, think of that!'

The other women — Mrs. Underhill with her eldest in the new war, Mrs. Thorpe and Mrs. Jones who had lost brothers and uncles in the first one — were shamed by the neighbour's indulgent tongue, but could not silence her with their stares, and did not know what to say when the veteran widow had stopped and sat weeping daintily to herself in pleasant oblivion on Martha's chesterfield. Mrs. Jones busied herself making tea; Mrs. Thorpe mentioned the good news in The Reporter about the imminent end to the War, then went red to the roots of her silver hair. Mrs. Underhill with some difficulty began talking about what a fine young man Guy junior was turning out to be.

Why do only the women come f was the crazy thought of

Martha Gibson. Where are the men? Do they not feel grief? Can they not give comfort as well? I have been without a man for five years. In the midst of my youth, my yearning, I have done without, and the anguish has been great. Now in my need for consolation I am left to the ministrations of these women who have lived the better half of their lives.

But Mrs. Taylor is right, was her second thought. She could read it in the eyes of the knowing around her. Mrs. Taylor might be foolish and unthinking, but she was not in disagreement with the other three women.

I will not believe. I won't. If there is one chance in a million that Guy is alive, then I will hold onto that. It may be small hope, but surely my love for Guy was no bigger than that when I spurned him all those months and he kept persisting, his ardour redoubling in the face of my every rebuff. How proud I was! And how happy to cast it all away, at last.

She would not believe. And she did not, for the entire six weeks that lay between then and now. But each day she began to see the import behind Mrs. Taylor's gratuitous cruelty. Better to accept the inevitable as far as possible, to re-order your own life, to get yourself prepared for the second telegram or what-is-worse the troop-train a year from now that holds no face for you standing on the platform among the grieving and jubilant. And while she never once, in speech or look, let on to Little Guy that there was anything but hope, she began, night by night, to entertain the idea of her husband's death. What kind of death? How did it differ from a five-year absence? In the whispering shade of their marriage- room, in the bed where their son had been conceived and re-conceived, Martha wondered how death could be anything more than the extension of absence. He would not return. That was it. But suppose he did. Would he be the same Guy who made love to her right here till night's end before boarding the long train for boot-camp?

Many girls in the village had been attracted to his handsomeness, his farm-boy's frame that fitted together awkwardly when at rest but flowed and articulated with breathless grace when moving in one of the arenas that could challenge it — the hockey rink, ball diamond, lacrosse box. Something in Martha resisted this, found more to love in the voice and eyes when they were settled and by themselves. Even on the ice Guy's heartiness and good cheer were legion. His voice called out encouragement or offered solace. He was the ultimate good-guy around the village. He whistled while he walked and hummed his way through the arduous days at the freight sheds. In the lilac evenings of late April, he was pursued by young women wanting to give or take — anything — in the presence of a spirit that was more than male and seemed too beautiful for use. Martha did not pursue. In the end he saw her as she was, though his pride (in his good nature) had to be shorn down against her own (fear of being loved without constraint). And she accepted his annihilating daily joy and turned it into something reborn through both of them every night.

In a year Little Guy was born. After three years, their happiness unquelled (though chastened by the child's impending presence), her husband abandoned her. At least that is how she remembered it, the only way she would ever remember her courtship and their deathless union.

But that much she had known before the telegram, even before the first of his weekly letters. That much would be altered by neither his death nor his return. Or would it? Would Guy Gibson — five years older, his goodness maimed by the horrors he hinted at in his letters and irretrievable even with her love — would he be able to shake her from this steadfast vision of how they had first loved and designated the future for themselves? It was possible.

She shivered. The water in the sink was stone-cold. It was quarter to seven. The music lesson.

Even so, his absence was a kind of death. A month after he had gone, despite the cheerful passion of his letters, she discovered how much their love depended upon his daily presence across the room from her and his gentle plundering of her body at night. For a few of her young friends, this sort of absence seemed a blessing: they were able to fantasize a love grander than their home-made beds would allow, were able to make their distant husbands talk for them and side with them and fill their dreams with the wicked scenes of unannounced furloughs. For Martha, whose marriage had been good, and very real (rooted in flesh, smile, caress), the absence of a partner was calamitous.

Not that she ever let on. Or admitted. Some did, carting their adultery discreetly across the Bridge into the States. No one had performed the act openly within the village. There was a war on. And a God who didn't take kindly to such accidents.

If Guy did not return? This kind of death, the feigned life she had been leading for five years, would also end. Widowhood. A year of mourning perhaps. And still not thirty. She could be no Mrs. Taylor. But what then? If Guy was gone (and how could she accept that) then the vision of their courtship and mating would be made permanent, would be an inerasible memory as chiselled on her dreams as Guy's name would be on the Monument. Oh God, how can I be thinking this, he's only missing in action f There might even be another. A different one. With some music in him, opening an untried, tentative, yearning being she would learn to recognize as herself.

Maybe this was all designed. Was a series of accidents not a design? Guy dead. Their marriage a rejuvenating memory. Little Guy, the image of his Dad, needing a real father. The mother, discovering that her flawless marriage has closed doors for both partners, chooses a new one for him and for herself. Not the original excitement — nothing will ever be like that again — but it will be new. Life is renewal: that's the design. I believe that.

Martha shuddered. Fear and guilt. And hope. One in a million. Oh God, Guy, be alive. I don't care if you come back and hate Little Guy and you can't smile except in the dark of our bed against my body, I don't care if the memory of our good years gets battered, I don't care because all of it — good and bad — will be alive and real and happening. If you die, I want to see it, and if I die, I want you beside me. I cannot cry into empty rooms, I want my weeping to be heard. I'll take even the pain of your rejection or the scorn of your shattered eyes — to this waiting. Yes, God, I have had wicked thoughts, my flesh has been weak, but You have no cause, You really don't. And I would give my right arm if you would send him back safe to me.

She was shaking all over. She mustn't let the teacher (she still called him that in her mind) see her like this. After all, nothing had happened. Nothing at all. He was a fine young gentleman who took his teaching seriously. He was always punctual and polite. Not once in slipping his pale, sculpturing fingers across her own to show her the fingering for a complicated section or in standing behind her turning the page with his musked cheek no more than an inch from her hair — not once did he appear anything but the gentleman. Not once.

She suspected, however, that it was more than politeness or sympathy that kept him sitting for almost an hour across from her in the front room — listening to her talk, so patient for his youth, and then in turn when he knew she had to have talk of some outside world, he would go on and on about music, about Bach and the organ, his piano training in Toronto, and his one summer in Vienna before the troubles began. He had stood in Beethoven's apartment and touched his pianoforte. Here was a world unknown (and uncared about) in the Point. Martha had taken piano as a girl. Her mother, from a 'fine' City family (respectable but poor), 'married down' to a rough but cheerful businessman from the County. She was ten when the lessons stopped and her mother died.

She needed these evenings, Tuesday and Friday; she needed the music. Why? It seemed so foolish: the neighbours raised the village brow, talked, grew more puzzled and yet (she hoped) remained as curious as skeptical. No one, yet, had any question that the new organist might offer romantic temptation to the grieving widow-to-be. He was young and scandalously skinny; she was older, upright, and scandalously attached to her husband.

Strange that with five years gone and this death-in-living, she found that she needed some other memory, deeper than the one that had been sustaining her. A more beautiful one, solitary, residing in the child-she-was and its more perfect correlation with the tiny swiss-watch movements of God's universe.

And all this before the telegram, before her own wayward thoughts. The movements of Cam Hornby's fingers across the keys soon became love's scripture, a code for their mating dance. The music stirred both memory and desire. Was past and future. Last Tuesday she had come close to pressing him to her right there on the chesterfield, wanting only the strength of his body and his youth, and to hell with all else. She had, for the sake of her desire, been ready to violate the most sacred contract the village held among its people as a social-group beleaguered by war. And would have except for the arrival of Little Guy. But would she really have done it? Was there not a part of her that knew exactly when cub scouts let out?

She knew only one thing for certain, even as she tidied up the room and set the music sheets on the piano; so long as Guy remained that one in a million who might be alive, she would be his wife, and pretend as long as need be that their life had been continuous and shared.

My right arm, I swear!

Chapter

4

THE HALL WAS FILLED by six fifty-five. The whole town was out — drawn by curiosity, boredom, a sense of impending excitement. Duff Gleason, who cleaned up after Lodge-night on Wednesdays, had got the day wrong, wandered into the throng with mop-and-pail, and decided to stay. For many it was a picnic in wintertime: the women gossiping in tight knots near the centre of the room (reef-knots, the Reeve punned to himself, delighted to find his wit keen); the men strung out along the walls like an undertrained platoon, joking with one neighbour then craning to hear a funnier one further down the ranks.

'The Reeve's in fine fettle tonight.'

'Got that suit from the Jew's in the City afore the War.'
'Which war?'

'Smells like it, too!'

Ha.

'No moths on him!'

Ha. Ha.

Let them have their little amusements. Served to warm them up, get them into the mood for the address of the decade. He could feel the speech inside him like a good drink; lying in there all cozied up: a bud of knowledge and power (dare he think glory?) waiting for his words to pull it into consequent bloom

35

(he'd try some fresh comparisons tonight: they were the heart of sermons and platform speeches, he knew from long experience).

In the audience he caught some of the faces which had special meaning for him. Charlie Brighton, who had fought alongside his brother, Edgar, and brought back the story of his brave and senseless death. (Charlie was trying to wink but ended up as usual squinting.) He saw that Red had made it after all, propped up as usual by his long-suffering wife. Now there was a loyal woman for you! He and Red had gone down to the recruiting centre together in 1915. Red was a good friend: not once had he worn his medal to show off or embarrass people who did not or could not get into the Service. The

Reeve nodded, and eased his baby finger along the sleeve of his best, double-breasted, herring-bone suit. He noted with mild displeasure that Guy's wife was absent and with some rueful pleasure that Quince was also among the truant.

'Hi ya, Reeve!'

Duff, waving his mop.

The Reeve of all the people waved back without prejudice.

* * *

BEFORE HIM on the meeting-table, spread with brand-new Maple-Leaf wallpaper, lay two sheets of foolscap and a thick binder. This was, after all, a kind of Council meeting, a sort of committee-of-the-whole you might say, and the details (his speech) would be duly taken and preserved in the official Minutes. Underneath his notes for tonight's address lay a paper whose contents would be revealed to only two people in the room. He marvelled at his own daring to bring it here, right out in the open.

My darling Gloria:

Denfield's bam. The loft. Friday evening next. Twelve midnight. Our joy begins. I am your Reeve for life.

Love,

Horace

On the other sheet he had printed the only notes he would need for his speech.

1. Hockey Game with Port Rangers next Friday (details)
2. Visit of Governor-General a week from Saturday (details)
3. Annex Incorpor Consolidation (some details)

He chanced a peek to his right where Gloria was sitting, pencil poised. She was ... glorious. A fixed blush on either cheek portending passion. Her agate eyes seized the weak light of the hall in their precious depth to be released only under a lover's touch. Her hair was the colour of straw in August: incendiary. Her lover: an arsonist. As he passed down the binder, she dared not look at him, but her fingers grazed the hair on the back of his hand — the hand which had just slipped the news of paradise into the page marked for tonight's minutes. She could not miss it.

He felt exuberant, heroic, positively Arthurian. He would not use his notes. He crumpled them into a ball and stuffed them into his herring-bone pocket.

Duff Gleason, all-round factotum, reached up and placed a pitcher of gleaming water beside the speaker. Chairman Wise cracked his gavel and a hush fell on the assembled village.

* * *

THE BOY WAS SEVEN. Beside him, his father: giant hands drooped like catcher's mitts out of the sleeves of his shiny suitcoat, Adam's apple bobbing above the celluloid collar, tie askew, sweat from the proud, grained forehead oozy as pine-sap. Hands that wielded the hammer without compassion, swung the sledge with ease, jumped to the saw's jig. Hands that cradled and whacked, one of them holding his own at this moment in a tender grip.

The crowd around them jostled and manoeuvred. Necks stretched, craned, went oblong — all eyes on the tracks near the dusty shanty with the white sign: green glades. He could see little but the sagging end of overalls, pressed trousers and the heels of scuffed, hastily polished boots. He didn't care. He was happy. He squeezed the callouses on his father's palm and felt the tremours rippling down to him through the awesome bones and savage musculature of the man he watched every Saturday among the sweet shavings and sawdust and humming heat. He closed his eyes; he was swinging the balpean, his father smiled as the nail died in the two- by-four.

'Here she comes!'

Some serious jockeying took place now that the puff-puffing of the locomotive could be heard down where the track curved at the edge of the hamlet. Some scuffling broke out. An ugly farmer in front of him farted and guffawed. His

father stood his ground and no one jostled them. He heard the train go by, screeching its brakes and tossing black confetti on the crowd.

'Goddam filthy railroads/ barked a man to their left.

'I'll take horseshit any day!'

'All I can say is this bugger better be worth me puttin' on a shirt and tie.'

He will, his father's hand, in his, replied.

'Okay Horrie, up you go!'

These were the first words he had spoken since they left home, and the boy's heart leapt to them and to the cradling hands that hoisted him high above the crowd and sat him on shoulders as wide as a dray's.

What he saw was even more amazing, in itself and because he could feel every tingle of response in his father's frame. The train had indeed passed by, but just far enough to leave the rear platform-car in full view of the expectant crowd. The coach was golden in hue with velvet curtains on the windows and gleaming brass lanterns on the back. The ornate railing around the little dias bounced sunlight. A scarlet banner floated above with a strange insignia on it like a secret code or password. He expected to see a king emerge through the burnished doors onto the red carpet and they would all sink to their knees.

A fat man in a black suit came out, puffing with the effort of getting the doors apart.

Cheers and applause.

'Boo!'

'Down with the Grits!'

'Throw the bums out!'

Louder cheers. Some scuffling. His father's knuckles going white. The boy winced, excited and appalled.

'Ladies and gentlemen of Green Glades!' boomed the fat black suit with the enthusiasm of a barker at a girlie-show.

'No gentlemen here!' hollered fart-face.

His father's hand left his and settled gently on the farmers shoulder. The man jerked around, paled, and held his peace.

'I give you the Prime Minister of the Dominion of Canada!'

The only sound was the rhythmic pant of the steam-engine.

Into the sunlight and silence stepped an arresting figure, immaculate in gray and white. He moved easily as if at home on red carpets before strange crowds in distant places. He raised his hands in a gesture that registered, for the onlookers, surprise, gratitude, humility, self-possession, and power.

Then he spoke. Neither the boy nor the crowd had heard such a voice, astounding in its range and depth as it poured from that tiny source. It was as if the man were expanding before their gaze — his gesticulating arms and his rhetorical eye rising up and out to keep pace with the words that shaped the air they rode upon, threatened to free themselves utterly, to find their own horizon.

He spoke of the great capital in Ottawa, of teeming cities east and west, of a country with oceans for borders, of wheat farms as vast as the Caspian sea, of forests wider than China, of lakes so numerous they could not be named with two languages; he spoke of the glorious past; and he reminded them that God had granted them the future.

The boy felt his father's dance through shoulder-bone, sensed the whole crowd lean, topple, rebound. He wanted to sing with his eyes closed forever.

On the way home his father said, 'That was Sir Wilfrid Laurier.'

Three months later the cancer had its way. The hardest thing the man who was the boy ever had to do was join the other Party. The easiest was to pick up the carpenter's tools and head for the nearest town.

* * *

THE REEVE WAS IN FULL FLIGHT. His voice was a kite in the north wind over the Bridge. It reared, kicked against the string, then soared beyond sight. He was still on the first item. The crowd was silent. Not a cough. All eyes on his rhetorical right hand as it fluttered and snapped stiff and dropped to half-mast — like spectators at a tennis match. His only wish was to be out there with them, listening.

During one of his dramatic pauses he reached down and took a huge quaff from the pitcher. My God! Uncut gin! His

face contorted as he searched for a place to swallow. The crowd, smelling a denouement, leaned forward. For several seconds no word could find a route through the fiery channel. Was it bad news after all?

But when the orator's voice returned and good news came, the villagers responded with one heart. At last, a real hockey game; that meant something; with bouyant winners and humiliated losers; their individual cheers would be uncompromised and necessary. The town saluted with twenty-one guns!

The Reeve staggered, sweat popped from his brow. He took a moment to glance over at Gloria Sawbush. She would have read the note by now. She smiled at him, struck by the same awe that had moved the rest of the village, but otherwise showed no sign of special knowledge. What a trooper she was! Able to control herself perfectly in what must be the most testing of circumstances. Yes, he had made the right choice. She was a woman to stand on podiums beside legislators, or premiers.

He took a sip of water and started in on the small details. A friendly game. Hands across the Bridge, he reminded them. Mayor Bulliant of the Port would be present. Yes, and a free banquet to follow, here in this very Hall. A trophy, too, to be presented by no less a personage than William Dougall MacAdorey.

'Three cheers for the Reeve!'
'Hip, hip, hurrah!'
There were no dissenters, not even a conscientious objector.

* * *

YES, THERE WAS A TIDE in the affairs of politicians, and the Reeve was riding its crest, here in the strangest of places: an obscure village on a timid peninsula poking out into a Lake which was vaster than half the so-called seas of the world, buttressed by one of the world's most powerful rivers, and bordered on one side by the menacing allure of the United States of America and on the other by the rapacious envy of the City; here in the strangest of times, with the world turning itself inside out, the old loyalties and brief certainties breaking asunder with every crack of the doomsday guns.

A second wave of adulation had just broken over the Reeve's already overtaxed shoulders. For a moment he teetered as if he would surrender to it, then caught his balance and let all that unalloyed joy and love and pride pour over him. The Governor-General? Yes, the Governor-General, that five-star British commander come straight from the King's privy chamber to Ottawa and thence straight to London and thence straight to the Point, not stopping in the City at all, mind you, but coming straight to the Monument with the dust of his desert campaigns fresh on his epaulettes and the royal scent still aromatic on the brow their King had blessed with his lips. And the very day after the game, when their hearts would be swelled with the pride of a local victory (and the righteousness of suppressed gloating). It was too much to believe, to even hope for, but a Reeve's word was unimpeachable. They had caught his rhetoric on the wing and it carried them high above the Bridge into the tall air where deep dreaming was yet possible. Or so it seemed, watching that double-breasted figure of manhood toss the phrases they needed to hear from the tips of his talking hands.

Redmond waved his silver flask like a banner.

The ladies' lace handkerchiefs caressed and incited.

Duff Gleason tattooed joy on his pail.

Charlie Brighton grinned, and his gold teeth glinted like DSO's.

Maxie Wise applauded with his eyes.

Little Guy Gibson raised his janitor's mop and gave a seven-gun salute.

The perfumed hair of Miss Sawbush ignited.

The crowd surged towards the cynosure of their happiness.

'Ladies and gentlemen, please,' said Chairman Wise, 'our Reeve hasn't finished.'

They would not be called to order. They mounted the dias like celebrants in a Victory-Day parade. Gavel, chairman, empty water-pitcher and secretary were capsized without ceremony.

'Reeve! Reeve! Reeve!' they chanted with more rhythm and conviction than they ever managed a Sunday-morning hymn.

Within seconds the choir-director was on their shoulders. Though firmly pinned between Charlie Brighton and Red Redmond, the Reeve seemed to be floating on the swell of the village itself.

'Hey, watch my suit — '

'Reeve! Reeve! Reeve!'

'Christ, you're tearing my — '

For he's a jolly good fellow
For he's a jolly good fellow
For he's a jolly good felloooooooo
Which nobody can deny

They were drifting towards the exit. With a purpose.

'Let's carry him home!'

Universal applause.

The Reeve felt the smack of the cold on his overheated cheeks. He rubbed the tear in his herring-bone pocket and tried to look nonchalant as he wobbled six feet above ground. What a triumph! Never in his ripest fantasy had he envisaged anything like this. His senses spun in the dizzying cold, but his heart was as big and as hot and as steady as any man could desire. He leaned back as they paddled past the Monument and aimed north on Michigan Ave. Where was Gloria? The soul-mate to share this moment. He caught a glimpse of her framed in the light of the doorway to the Hall, her gaze fixed on her man; she smiled as she saw him turn, and he was certain that in it he read a sign which could only be called conspiratorial.

* * *

IT WAS NOT until the congregation — puffing and shivering and somewhat less trembling with delerium — deposited him on the throne of his verandah that the Reeve remembered he had forgotten to say something that was somehow crucial to the evening and the events to follow. Well, no matter. One does not worry the general with small details on the eve of his mightiest campaign.

* * *

'YOU'RE EARLY, DEAR,' said Quince from the chesterfield.

'I got a lift home,' he grinned inwardly. Not even she could sour his spirits this evening.

'I've just about finished these Argyle socks. I'll only be a minute. Would you like a game of hearts?'

'Ah, no. I have a lot of work to do. Small details for next weekend, you know.'

She didn't but said: 'I understand, dear. Maybe I'll just start another pair.'

'Don't you ever get sick of doing that?' Now where did that come from?

Quince was shocked. 'It's for the boys.'

'Ah, yes, the cause.' The goddam bloody cause.

'Oh, my dear, you've caught your suitcoat pocket on a nail.'

'I hadn't noticed.'

'That drafty old Hall's a disgrace. Well, no matter, just leave it here and I'll fix it next week.'

'I'll need it by Wednesday. I'm meeting with Mayor Bulliant. And on Thursday I meet with Mr. MacAdorey,' he said with as much casualness as he could muster.

'Oh. Well, I think I can manage that all right, dear. I've only got three more pair of socks to finish up before the bee next Thursday.'

Think? My God, you see what I have put up with all these years?

Gloria. Gloria Sawbush.

Chapter

5

'GOOD EVENING, Mrs. Gibson.'

'You're early, Mr. Hornby. Do come in.'

'I've brought some new music.'

'How lovely. Thank you.'

Door closing on the cold. The neighbours: deliberately not watching. The snow: a giant muffler, a host for all voices, random or calculating.

* * *

MR. HORNBY — Cam — was once again in her front room, a presence both familiar and exotic, comforting and intoxicant. She always fussed about him — coat, scarf, fedora, galoshes — making him nervous no doubt. More motherly than intended.

'It's all right, Mrs. Gibson, I can manage the coat, thank you,' he said, his voice alto and formally cadenced, as if he had acquired it outright at the Conservatory. But she had both hands on the coat, drawing it deliberately away from his narrow, esthetic shoulders. She hung it on the hall stand next to his handsome fedora, smelling the cold and warmth of it, while he removed his felt overshoes with more grace than a village deserved. She felt her breath lodge in her throat: he was like a gazelle. That was always the image through which she beheld him and recalled him later. Tall, and made taller by his slimness and the fit of his dark suit; the arms always in motion at the end of which floated, in practised harmony, his pianist's hands. Whenever he was at rest, in the olive chair next to the chesterfield or across from her at the kitchen table over coffee, he possessed that animal's nervous energy — his brown eyes darting, on edge, unsure of their surroundings, though the voice remained musical and certain. However, when he took the piano-bench, alone or beside her, that energy flowed steadily from some indetectable centre outward to the limbs and in flawless synchronization to the distant power in the marvellous white fingers against the keyboard. At night, reliving a Tuesday or Friday, she could never recall his face, neither its individual features (which were sharp and memorable) nor its bright, fluctuating moods — she could recreate only that gazelle-like expression of energy and grace, the inexhaustible shapes that his hands made and remade, and the passion stored in the mysterious source quickening them.

'Would you like to go over Tuesday's lesson?'

'Later, if you don't mind. I'd like to hear you play for a while.'

'But you play very well, you know.'

'Please. I've had a rather bad day.'

'No news?' He could not say 'good' or 'bad'.

'No. No news.'

'It must be terrible for you.'

'I'm not alone. There are others.'

'Yes. Too many. But you don't deserve — '

'Mrs. Baker is a widow, you know. Tommy was — is her only son. She's been waiting nearly four months.'

'T didn't know.'

'I have Little Guy.' And where was Little Guy right now? Twice he had been escorted home after the eight o'clock curfew. She had to get hold of herself. Soon.

'But you must hope, Martha.'

He called her Martha. He was blushing, his eyes searching for a place to alight.

'I do hope ... Cam. I live on it. But some days ...'

'I know. Oh, Mrs. Gibson, I wish I did know. I feel so out of place, sometimes, here. Coming in from the big city where all of this is so — so anonymous. Sitting in the loft Sunday after Sunday, watching the eyes of the widows, and the mothers who are going through this for a second time. I am a stranger in their midst, playing the hymns they still believe in. I wonder how they can. They have a strength I want to know about. I am so young — '

'But you give them your music, Cam. That is a wonderful and selfless thing.'

'Oh no, I cannot see it that way. It is very selfish, music. I feel it is my protection, a place for me to hide and comfort myself.'

Her heart was skipping beats. She must control it, she must not let him see. But oh how he could talk! There was no one, now or then, who could talk like Cam Hornby. His heart was unfettered, like his music, and she sensed he would speak like this in no other room.

'And you have such a way with children. Eighteen pupils, we've never had so many taking piano. And the Boys' Band, too. Already you are ... loved.'

'I am building on the twenty-years' labour of Mr. Evans, God rest his soul.'

'But it is important work. You must believe, Cam.'

'As you must hope?'

She felt the force of his wry smile. Her hand shook and she

grasped the piano-bench.

'Will you play?'

'Well, I did bring some Chopin.' He flushed, and again she was struck by the terrifying innocence of his glance. What was she doing? Some field in France, this very moment, might be reclaiming the ripped flesh of her husband.

'Please,' she heard herself say.

* * *

SHE FELT ODDLY SECURE now that music filled the room, expanding it, and she could sit passive on the chesterfield to listen and to watch Cam Hornby's fingers stroking the keys. She had no sense that these instruments belonged to the boy/man with a voice and a troubled heart and a private aloneness. They constructed the music on their own like sculptor's hands against glittering marble, all passion transmuted to the form itself. But what passion in these études she had not heard or remembered since her mother played them to herself in her last days, the child unloved in the corner transfixed and resentful — she felt the heart in them; its anonymous longing, its breaking and mending and breaking; the random, terrible love driving them nameless and homeless to the brink. 'Again,' she breathed.

* * *

'I ALWAYS WANTED to be a concert pianist, you know. My mother took me to Vienna in the summer of thirty-seven when I was fifteen. They told me there that I had talent. I practised eight hours a day. We had a little flat near St. Stephens. I would go out at night by myself and look at the cathedral. Centuries old. And it was like a kind of music, you know. I can't really explain it because I am not very good at that sort of thing, but it was a feeling I had every time I saw it, like those architects and stonemasons were working from a score in their hearts, or in their souls because it was a religious music that carried them through the years it took to create the ageless structure. I believed very strongly then, much more than I can now. I didn't know at the time we were surrounded by guns and tanks and men who hated music.'

'Go on. Please.'

'Of course we had to leave. My professor was a Jew. One day he simply was not there when I came for my lesson. They were getting ready to sell his piano.'

'You were so young, then.'

'Yes. I took one of his scores, with his name on it. Chopin. I still have it.'

'I know.'

* * *

'i should go.'

'Still ten minutes to curfew.' Little Guy was never home before curfew.

'I really should, you know.'

'I haven't played my piece for you.'

'Do you want to?'

'No.'

* * *

'I'LL ASK CHIEF PIERSALL to look for him.'

'He'll be home. Don't worry.'

50

They were at the door. It was warm in the room. He turned towards the windless cold. Struggling with his gloves.

'Cam!'

Her hands were in his, tiny and powerless. She felt the residual tremors in him.

'You are a very special person.'

'You'll come next Tuesday?'

'Perhaps I shouldn't.'

'I'll practice, I promise.'

He smiled and was gone.

Oh Guy, where are you? My right arm, I promise.

Chapter

6

'THE THORPES'VE GONE over to the Groceteria. Think of that, Sarah.'

'What's the world coming to, Rose? I really don't know.' 'Seems to me we need all the loyalty we can get these days.' 'Well, they ain't got kith nor kin overseas.'

'But the mister was in the First One, you know.'

'Still, it's a disgrace.'

'What would they've done all through the Depression days without Red Redmond to give them credit, I'd like to know?' 'And him delivering every day, right to a body's door.'

The mistresses Underhill and Jones, on a bright Monday morning, were standing outside Redmond's Grocery, a bag tucked in the crook of an arm.

'Now the Reeve. There's loyalty for you.'

'There's a man indeed.'

'Guess I'll have to get out my blue satin.'

'Imagine, a genuine Governor-General, right here in the Point.'

'Almost like royalty when you come to think of it.'

'Ain't been royalty in this town since the Prince of Wales come humpteen years ago.'

'Takes a man like the Reeve to do that.'

'You wouldn't catch him going over to no Gro-ce-ter-ia!' They chatted on, walking a bit, letting the morning take care of itself, shifting arms every now and then.

'That Marg Redmond's all right, too, you know.'

'Heart of gold.'

'And smart as a whip with the figures.'

'Miss Jeremy says he takes a wee drop now and then.'

'She's a shameless gossip, that woman.'

'Got nothing else to do.'

'I don't approve of the drink, mind you. But after all's said and done, he's a good worker.'

'And loves the children.'

'Funny they never had any of their own, after that one ...' 'To each his own is what I always say.'

'Funny, all the same.'

Before parting in front of the Underhill house, they exchanged ration stamps without spilling an onion from either bag.

Mrs. Jones had a sweet tooth. The Underhill boys craved hamburger.

It would be nice to be the Redmonds — owning your own grocery.

Chapter

7

MONDAY MORNING. Garbage day. A fresh week. The Reeve was trying to convince his skeptical bones that it was in fact to be more than an ordinary week. They were heading into good times. Cranking the engine of his equally skeptical truck, he cast about for auguries.

The weather was holding. The sun shone as if it mattered. The sky was February blue. The cold: dismembering but still. The snow lay quiescent where the Reeve's imagination had placed it.

'Come on, Edgar ol* boy. You're in this, too,' he urged, flipping the crank handle.

Edgar coughed, inhaled, became a believer.

'Good old chap.'

He had bruised only one knuckle. The signs were good. Like the times.

* * *

NO HELPER. What a day for Duff Gleason to come down with lumbago — of the brain, he thought and then immediately chastised himself for want of charity. However, moments later when he wheeled into Pott's Lane and saw the piles of trash and

54

reeking garbage awaiting him, his charity lost some of its edge. If he has a brain!

What an indignity for a man of his sensibility to endure. This very week he would be meeting with Mayor Bulliant of the Port — a former us Senator, no less — and with William Dougall MacAdorey, confidant of premiers and vice-regals; he would be presiding over an international banquet vital to the morale of the Home Front; he would be standing on the same flag-draped podium as the King's surrogate, representing his people and their vast hopes. And he had just caught his royal handshake between the truck-box and Wollochuk's garbage can!

Judas priest! If his mother had a brain!

The pain sizzled like a string of ladyfinger firecrackers all

the way to his right elbow. Wounded in action, he thought, amazed at his wit and good humour under fire. He was still congratulating himself when the last bag of Wollochuk flotsam (which had been teetering unmolested on the edge of the truck) washed ashore, all over the Reeve's best mackinaw.

Was that old Wollochuk in his shanty-window grinning at him, gums aglow, as he brushed off potato peels, coffee grounds and last night's garlic? Polack crap on the town's first citizen! Well, they would soon learn to miss him. There would be no more immigration when Horace Macintosh took power. He'd find a used cow-boat and send them all packing to the Salami Islands. Chanty, chanty.

Back in the warmth of the cab, he let the heater thaw the pain in his right hand. After all, these people were merely ignorant not malicious. He himself did not believe the rumours of their being agents provocative; he was above that sort of petty speculation. But damn-it-all they were a dumb bunch. Not one of them could speak the English language with any eloquence after thirty years here. And why in hell didn't they get decent jobs at the Foundry like everybody else and move their garlic breath out of these tumbledown three- storey shacks? What would the Governor-General think?

On the other hand, he mused philosophically as the truck barely missed a direct hit on Grogan's outhouse, that stupid veteran of the Boor War was white and English and yet lived right down here among them at the end of Pott's Lane. How could that be explained to a five-star general who spoke effortless English? And how could anyone explain why the one-armed son-of-a-bitch built his outhouse a foot from the side of his driveway, in his front yard? He couldn't accept the excuse that Grogan's family had always lived there, in better times, and that the privy had been converted from a tool-shed when its cousin sank in the quicksand behind the house. The whole town would have cheered if the Bandit had gone down with his ship.

Well, maybe he would just quit cleaning the snow out of the old stump-waver's driveway altogether. For years now he had refused to clear any of the walks or drives along Pott's Lane, ever since he had run over a cache of beer-cases at Blinski's.

But since Grogan's hovel was at the end of the dead-end street, he found it convenient to turn the truck around in there (not, as the Uke's claimed, because Grogan was the lone aristocrat on the block). But one of these days he'd just make a sharp left when his Nibs was plunk on the pot and rid the village of two eye-sores at once. Charity; these are new times.

He had just stopped in front of Marovitch's when he remembered which part of the Friday-night throne-speech he had forgotten to append.

He slumped over the wheel, in a daze.

Above him, the auguries spun like bats against the sun.

* * *

CONSOLIDATION. My God, how could he have forgotten that, of all things? He had shaken hands on it. A binding contract the Party would hold him to. As a lifelong politician he knew how sacred such a handshake was. Without deals, under the table over brandy, where would they be in this province, in this country? He had to see MacAdorey on Thursday afternoon to confirm arrangements. With a flick of his Cuban cigar that potentate could alter the itinerary. After all, the City had a monument, too, a bigger one, even if it wasn't as impressive as theirs.

But more than the loss of a Governor-General was at stake here. Careers were made and broken on such issues. Rising stars and their co-respondents had tripped on tinier banana peels. What would Gloria think? Would she stand by him? Of course. That pact had already been sealed, and would be duly consummated this coming Friday in Denfield's loft. He needed to see her. Now. But the way his luck was running he hadn't been surprised to learn on Sunday that her bigwig father had returned to the City for a week, rented a fancy apartment and hauled her down there for a few days as decoration for his salon. But she had seen his note. Yes, her parting smile had been conspiratorial. She would be there, faithful innocent that she was. And what would her lover have to tell her, after their lofty bonding?

What, indeed. Pull up your galoshes, Macintosh. You're no callow youth. You've been seasoned in time: two wars and a depression have not borne you down. You're a survivor, a combatant. And who is William Dougall MacAdorey anyway? The whole Party? Is there not a County seat north of here, where I was born and raised, desperate for a quality candidate?

With Gloria, anything seemed possible. Besides, a cog in the gears of time had inexorably clicked over. He was too much in his prime to turn back. With a flourish, he flipped open the cab and hopped to the street. The confident slam of the truck-door jarred the slumber of every un-Canadian on Pott's Lane.

* * *

WHEN THE REEVE tipped Marovitch's garbage pail over the edge, the contents clinked and shattered. Liquor bottles. Three or four dozen of them. He must speak to Chief Piersall about the unconscionable number of private 'parties' held in that house. No one, it seemed, had ever seen old man Marovitch buy a single mickey of vodka at the Liquor Control. You'd think he was a teetotaler. Where, then, did he get the stuff? 'They're bring-your-own-bottle parties,' Maxie Wise had suggested. Sure, and that's how the old Uke prospered without working a day in his life — selling salami sandwiches to his 'guests'! Some guests! The riff-raff of the town mixing without shame with these foreigners who would never fit into normal village life if they lived here a hundred years. And what a house for a party — once a three-storey, thriving hotel serving the railroad trade before the City with the treacherous aid of Cap Dowling got control of the Grand Trunk and left the village high and dry; now a ramshackle ruin that looked as if it were being occupied by refugees from an air-raid. Had they no civic pride?

And that daughter of Marovitch's: a pretty girl for a foreigner, and bright too, they said: running off to the Collegiate in the City and running around with every young scamp in town. Well, what else could be expected with a bootlegger for a father? And though he never gave credence to rumour, he saw no reason to doubt the story behind her sudden removal to a so-called aunt's house in Stratford. The story needed no rumour to embellish its sordid detail.

This town, the Reeve concluded, needed something to raise its morale and its morals. Whatever he was to tell Mr. MacAdorey on Thursday, it must not jeopardize the game or the visit. Too much was at stake. Civilizations rose and fell. The future of this village lay squarely and heavily on his broad, garbage-besmirched shoulders.

He dumped Marovitch's second can onto the shards of the first. At least it was conventional trash. But in among the peelings and wrappers, a familiar object caught his eye. With the thumb and forefinger of his left hand he drew it out into the shame of the February sun.

Duff Gleason's baseball cap, the one he wore summer and winter.

Lumbago indeed.

Chapter

8

AFTER LAST WEEK'S STORM, the sky had returned to them. Dazzling by day, the sun poured all its repressed heat into furious light. At night the stars, rinsed white, glistened like a farther, more pure form of snow. The moon widened towards perfection in the absolute blackness, giving just enough light to the dozen village-boys on the pond-ice below.

Surrounded by four-foot snowbanks laboriously shovelled after each snowfall of the long winter, these waifs were able with little effort to imagine that the clearing in the swamp beside the Bridge was their arena. And who was to say that these filigree figures, circling and gliding, blurred as they were by shadow and half-light, were not Maple Leafs or Canadiens? Certainly not Little Guy standing between the paint cans at the north end, borrowed goal stick in hand and eyes fastened on the black disc skittering from blade to blade before him. No matter even that he was skateless (his mother forbade him to play hockey in the dark — 'It's too dangerous, dear, you could trip on anything down in that swamp').

'Pass it! Pass it!'

'Johnny, over here! Come on!'

'Oww — '

'I said no raising, Wollochuk!'

'It hit a stick.'

'Once more and I'm going.'

'Who gives a damn!'

'It's my goalie stick, Orie, I'm warning you.'

'Off the post! No goal, you guys!'

'Right in! Three to two!'

'Three to three!'

The Indian whoops of their joy and anger rose with the clash of sticks and irregular ack-ack of rubber on wood. Fifteen minutes to curfew.

'Hey, here come the big guys! The team!'

Not quite all, but three of them at least: the Underhill brothers and Skinny McKeough, the entire first line of the Flyers. Little Guy watched in awe as they stepped through

the path in the bank at his end — fresh from their evening practice at the Rink two blocks away. And still in uniform, with their pads bulging like armour under their blue stockings and jerseys, and the moonlight dazzling on their white hockey-pants.

'Mind if we play,' laughed McKeough, winking at Brian and Fred Underhill. It wasn't a question.

'Maybe they can show us a thing or two,' said Fred.

Little Guy heard their skates bite the ice with a sound that sent tingles along his backbone; in three strides they were in high flight, cutting in and out of the younger boys who seemed to be standing still or turning in dazed circles. The entire rink began to shrink before his eyes as he followed, breathless, their surging momentum. Round and round they flew, widening the circuit each time till their skates came within an inch of the four banks. Then they picked up a loose puck and began passing it briskly in a dizzying series of patterns, their sticks brandished like ancient weapons, their cries menacing, thrilling, wordless.

McKeough, with no warning, drilled a low shot which no one saw but everyone heard: bruising air and driving deep into the south bank with a muffled explosion.

'Hey, that's our only puck,' he heard Orie yell.

McKeough didn't answer; he had turned, shifted gears and with just the slightest flick of his left hip caught Orie Wollochuk and sent him sprawling into the snow. What a check! And he never broke the rhythm of his threshing stride. As if on cue, the Underhills wheeled and bowled over Johnny MacArthur and Fatty Tate. Fatty spun around twice, one leg in the air and looking for land, and then crashed down on his face. It was like the Big Leagues! Little Guy felt the breeze on his face as McKeough swerved past him, then ground to a stop in a spray of ice flung up like smoke from a mortar. There was no fear in Little Guy, only a marvelling sense of the gratuitous power in those legs, that armoured body and its cold precision.

McKeough flipped a regulation-size puck on the ice and yelled, 'Okay, Undie-hills, it's us against them!'

And the chase was on — eleven would-be Flyers in hot pursuit. They didn't ask Little Guy to play goal, he merely stayed where he was. For five minutes no one touched the puck but the genuine Flyers as they passed, stickhandled and bodied their way through the enemy formations, soon left demoralized and in disarray. Their skating was neither as swift nor as clever as their hopes.

'Hey, no raising!'

'Hey, no raising!' mimicked an Undie-hill.

Twice more his pal Orie went tumbling to the ice and staggered up, red-faced and raging with a kind of wild joy. For Little Guy it was better than Maple Leaf Gardens and he never once took his gaze from the one warrior who manoeuvred like

Prometheus among midgets. Which is why he was the first to notice the titan change from his looping and deking to a straight drive over the 'blue-line', splitting the defence (one east, one west) and firing without aim. Little Guy did not see the shot that felled him.

'You raised it! You raised it!'

'Are you okay, Guy?' Orie asked, halfway between anxiety and awe.

Tears spurted from the goalie's eyes, but he wasn't crying. He really wasn't.

'It's — it's all right, it got the back of my leg, that's all.' Ten boys looked for the back of his leg. Little Guy couldn't feel it anyway, it was numb. Through the treacherous tears he was looking for some other kind of comfort.

'You lost the puck again,' Johnny complained, fishing in the bank behind them.

But Little Guy could see that the magnificent loser- of-pucks was not close enough to hear. All three Flyers had skated back to their own end and were buzzing in circles, waiting it seemed for the fuss to be over. The Underhills were laughing in great spurts between breaths.

'Hey,' called Orie, 'you really hurt this little kid, you know!'

Orie, no; please, not that way.

The great goalie was on his feet, but his right calf was still numb and he toppled over, burning with anger and shame. Orie had him by the shoulder, still glaring down-ice at McKeough, who, as if on a signal from his cohorts, skated towards the confused knot of boys at the north end of the swamp. The moonlight caught him from behind and cast a huge inflated shadow before him — looming, and dwarfing the figure from which it gathered its progressively sinister shaplessness. Only one of the boys was not riveted to that nether dance.

'Hey!'

McKeough covered them with the dust of a jarring stop.

'Somebody get hurt here?'

Little Guy's eyes brimmed with tears, and this time he was not crying.

'Naw. It's nothing, just a — '

'For Christ sakes, he ain't even got skates on!'

The Under-twins guffawed, and it was heard from south to north.

McKeough, from his gladiatorial height, glanced down at Little Guy, caught his worshipping eye, and snapped:

'You'll never make it, kid.'

* * *

'COME ON, GUY.'

'No, I gotta go. It's past curfew.'

'To hell with curfew. You missed it before.'

'I don't feel so good. I wanna go home.'

'Jeez, you can't let a prick like that get to you. Who the hell's he anyway?'

'My mom worries ... about Piersall.'

'They'd never make the team, not one of them, if their brothers wasn't in the War. Come on, there's lots of things to do. I feel like having some fun.'

'But Piersall — '

'We'll stick a firecracker in his jock-strap and tell him to count to ten!'

* * *

'THERE HE GOES.'

'Are you sure it's him?'

'Hell, that's him.' They were crouched in the laneway between the Richmond House and Maxie Wise's pool room.

Sure enough, the broad figure of the law, with a policeman's instinct for caution, glanced nervously about for several seconds, then marched straight into the Men's Room where he could keep a close eye on most of the miscreants of the village.

'What'll we do?'

'Let's wait for the drunks to come out.'

'Ahh...'

'Come on, let's get our ammunition.'

Even the moon did not betray the two commandoes reconnoitering the ammo-dumps of Richmond's alley.

Chapter

9

MARTHA WAS GLAD the telegram came just after supper. After dark. Not that the neighbours hadn't seen the taxi (Mrs. Taylor's lace peephole had hung open for a tense minute), but they wouldn't come now until morning. And Little Guy — Guy — had gone off to the swamp again. She had noticed his skates were missing from his peg and had not cared. How could she talk like this? Fussing over the busybody, wonderful neighbours and noticing trivial things like the boy's skates? Guy was dead. The War was over.

Still, it would be easier in the morning. To tell Little — Guy. To find the right face for the veteran widows. Time to open the telegram, sitting on the vanity unopened with full claim on its terrible knowledge. She could not bring herself to the point of looking directly at his death. Would it make any difference at all? Already she had watched him die countless times in the tearful, long nights here on this bed. And each death a different one, more horrible and maiming than the last — waking her upright in the gloom, cold sweat mixing too simply with the tears. She had been widowed so often that the tears, if they ever came again, would have no meaning for her. What would Mrs. Taylor think of that? What news of her callousness, her treachery, would be spread through the rumour-mills of the village?

66

If she had thought that opening the telegram would have made her cry, then she would have done so. In the morning perhaps. Before the visitations. Her worst thought at this moment, besides telling the child that the father he barely remembered had deserted him, was the anguish of the coming night when she would have to choose one of the images of slaughter from amongst the many. She would have to choose, to fix it once and for all; to set it in time and place forever; to give it some flesh she could cleave to, some permanent agony she could shore her grief against; some recurrable memory she could gradually learn to forget or resurrect at future moments of other grief when weeping would be called for. Then she would be able to set it comfortably into the common story of their lives that was now at last concluded. They met; courted; loved with abandon; conceived a son; parted heroically; exchanged passionate, death-resisting letters; and ...

And what? How long could you play the grieving widow to the village chorus? It isn't fair. I will not become Mrs. Taylor. Not for them. Not for myself.

How could she think like this, with Guy dismembered and unburied in some hell-hole? Her body should be torn asunder with sobbing. She should feel his soul in this room, at this hour. Memories of their lovemaking on this bed should be flooding her grief, assuaging it with bitter sweetness.

The clock ticked. A mouse turned over in the wainscotting. The sealed telegram waited.

Why did you leave me, Guy? It's not fair.

It never is, said her mother's voice; God works in His own ways, in His own time.

A knock on the front door. Not now, please.

A discreet tapping. Not Mrs. Taylor, or worse, the Reverend

Budge. She slipped the telegram into the vanity drawer. Maybe if she just saw someone, anyone, it would start. By the front door she saw Little Guy's skates where the boy had abandoned them at the last moment. Her heart lurched.

'Good evening, Martha.'

It was Tuesday. For two hours she had forgotten what had occupied her thoughts for four days.

'Are you all right? I can come back — '

'No, I'm fine. Come in, Cam.'

* * *

THE MOON, nearing its perfect circumference, poured a muted gold in through the half-shut curtains, casting an unblemished beam upon the naked bodies so recently disengaged from lovemaking. It caught in bold outline the breasts and hips of the woman. It softened and blurred in the young man's hunched shyness. The room was quiet. It might have been snowing.

Martha did not want to speak. She felt as if she had just reclaimed her body. Without moving she could see her toes, the tender skin between them; she could feel the blood mellow in her calves, warm on the undersides of her thighs, oozing heat from the harbour of her loins; she breathed the moonlight folded on her breasts. Her skin reached out to caress the cold. Her eyes drank the darkness around them.

She let the snow fall, unannounced.

Cam had been torn between desire and duty. She had to move his hands for him, introduce them to the forbidden parts of her flesh till they gained a momentum of their own. Slowly, patiently she guided them to autonomy. They held her at last, bent her breasts to their key, stirred the melody hidden and seeking within. She resisted, pressing him back, shaping his ardour to her necessity, squeezing the youth out of him.

It had been too long. He drove into her, unstrung and adolescent. She surrendered and thrived.

He came apart in the clenched nub of her. And too soon. The music in his hands, loins, tangled. He was elbows and knees and spent sweat. She clutched him then — fiercely, jangling, jerking him alive — to the centre of her desperation. They heaved and jarred together in the bereaved dark. She took what she needed. Powerless, he touched the dark tune within. Her cry stunned him, like a flower blown apart with light.

In her dream she was a butterfly immortalized by a boulder.

* * *

'CAM?'

His back, blocking the moonlight, shuddered with the sobs refusing to be released.

'Darling?'

The delicate hands held his face like a porcelain cup. Trembled. She reached out without turning; touched him along the shoulder, down the spine — strumming him.

'It was beautiful. Really.'

'I had no right,' he said, mostly to himself.

'We're lovers.'

'I'll make it right,' he continued, shifting to look for his clothes. 'I'll — I'll leave. Tomorrow. No one will ever know. I promise.'

'You must promise to love me.'

'You're a good woman. I had no right at all.' He found his underwear.

'You silly man. It was me who took you for a lover.'

'No, don't get up, please. I don't want to — to look at you. I'll leave. Now.'

Deliberately she slid into the moon's path, letting its glow stroke and melt where it would. For a second she saw her own image, felt the first shudder of regret, of guilt at what she had just done; what irreversible sundering of the boy's innocence she had accomplished, what calamity she had raised in her own conscience. He glanced up. Her nakedness was absolute.

'But your husband? Your child? What have we done?'

She did not reply. The vanity drawer drew open.

'My husband is dead,' she whispered, covering him, without regret.

The telegram, still sealed, lay half in shadow, half in light.

* * *

THIS TIME they did not disengage. They lay in one another's arms, adrift.

She let him soften in her, did not let go even then. Possession must be complete. The terrors, now, lay beyond this room, in the daylight. There was a lifetime for regret.

Her lover stirred. They made love with the patience of the ages, the urgency of the times. She closed her eyes. Tight. Like her wedding night. The wings of a familiar presence brushed them open.

Yes, my darling. I forgive you.

* * *

CAM WAS SMOKING, sitting on the bedside in Guy's old

bathrobe. Martha lay back on two pillows listening to the easy cadence of his voice.

'My father went broke, you see. Just after we got back. Lost the business. My mother begged and begged, but there was just no money. I went to UofT. Music education. The organ. This is only my second job.'

He kept his voice low, afraid the boy would be awakened. He never did, though, even if he had to wet the bed. Determined he was, like his father.

She began to weep. She was held.

* * *

IT WAS CAM who first heard the noise.

'It's a taxi, outside the Underhills.'

No. Not young Bill.

'Don't look, please. Not tonight.'

He came back, uncertain.

'What in God's name are they doing over there?' he cried out. 'Will none of us survive?'

'What's that?'

'A knock.'

'But that's our door!'

* * *

CAM WAS STRUGGLING into his clothes.

She left him and went into the front room, drained of all thought, all feeling. She unlatched the bolt, put on the porch-light, and let the door swing slowly open.

The doorway was filled with the figure of a large man, in

uniform, the khaki collar turned up against the chill, the wedge-cap pulled down over the forehead.

Martha looked directly into his eyes. He grinned, ear to ear. Then something drew her gaze downward: a crutch, under the right shoulder running down into the packed snow on the porch. One pantleg, turned under at the knee, swung freely in the space beneath the greatcoat.

'Guy?'

'You look surprised, sweetheart!' he said with the same, unchangeable good cheer. 'Didn't you get my telegram?'

Chapter

10

'IT'S HAPPY HARRY. Wow!'

'My leg's sore, Orie.'

'Jeez, what luck! Come on, get behind the bank.' Orie's eyes glinted and stretched as he ran his hands over the ammo.

It was definitely Happy Harry. You heard him before you saw him because he talked to himself when he was sober and sang to himself when he was drunk. Tonight he was drunk, and because he was also half-deaf, the pitch was operatic. Harry Bartholomew sang for his sanity in several overlapping keys; the lyrics were intricate and heartfelt though rendered in a language no one in the village could decipher. Shell-shock was the verdict: on the Somme, July 1, 1916 (though older residents claimed that he was 'never right to begin with'). He lived on Front Street only two blocks from his favourite bistro in a house that was 'a disgrace' about which 'something ought to be done' but never was. Harry spent most of his time in the warm seasons collecting old furniture, for re-sale it was assumed, and displaying it in the ample showroom of his front yard. He had a particular liking for things metallic: ice-boxes, stoves, ranges, Quebec heaters and chesterfields with wire-springs breathing freely through them. Since few customers ever came — Mrs. Thorpe had bought a gas-range in 1920, she said — the showroom became overstocked, and some items had to be placed on end or on top of a close cousin, even though their display value might be compromised. Some even rusted when the roof leaked. Finally Harry was compelled to cart some of the less attractive (non- metallic) pieces away to the dump, loading them by himself onto a sort of half-trolley/half-wagon he had confected out of some of the less saleable items, and hauling it, singing, to the Dump. In December the snow fell graciously upon each piece, turning the summer showroom into a winter garden which some people admitted to themselves was not unattractive. As for Harry, he talked his way to the Richmond every afternoon, sang his way home, and waited for warm weather.

Happy Harry was in no hurry. He had no watch. The song was swelling within him, voices that might have been his: clanging together in a wordless fugue. His head felt like a cathedral, like a canticle in a belfry.

'Yaaaaah, get him!'

'Eeeerrrraaaaa... attattatat!'

They heaved their snowballs, two in each hand, then reached down to their cache, instantly reloading. The enemy went down with the first volley, a direct hit to the forehead. The barrage continued, wave upon wave. Then stopped.

The commandoes had already turned to make their orderly retreat, convinced the wounds had been mortal, when they stood up simultaneously at rigid attention like puppies jerked on a choke-chain.

'Oh mygod mygod mygod mygod mygodmygod-MYGOD — '

On and on it went, a keening palinode that was only part-human and yet could be uttered by no creature other than man who can look across no-mans-land and see the image of his own hopelessness and be unable to go mad as the big guns open up along the Somme.

Chapter

11

IT WAS AUTUMN. Salvia in the garden. Goldenrod hugging the ditches. Wild phlox in the grottoes of First Bush.

The Reeve hummed a tune not quite in counterpoint with the engine of the dump-truck/snow-plough/garbage collector.

* * *

Dance with the dolly with the hole in her stocking
And her knees keep a-knocking
And her toes keep a-rocking
Dance by the light of the mooooooon!

It had been a good day on the garbage run. Duff Gleason, the town fool, who had driven the village bus for all the glorious sporting excursions before the War, had fallen on hard times. His bus on blocks in front of Merriman's garage, Duff had gone 'on relief', and the Reeve insisted that all able-bodied men work for their weekly dole. A political mistake in Duff's case. Today, however, they had managed to collect one hundred and sixty-two bags of garbage without spilling more than a dozen or so on the undefended village boulevards. And Duff, his left cheek swollen with toothache had not been able to talk to his driver /

supervisor — he merely uttered a continuous demi-whine which the Reeve found quite pleasant, even hum-inducing.

'You gotta let me off at the dentist's, Reeve!' Duff spluttered with lop-sided passion. 'The pain's killing me!'

The Reeve let that remark pass. Allowing his compassion to overrule his sense of propriety, he stopped the dump-truck in front of Marovitch's. The lawn as usual was untended, remnants of ragweed and lesser summer breeds aging in the Indian summer without shame.

'Watch out for the laughing gas!' called the Reeve. Duff had already disappeared through the tangle of hedges.

Well, he was alone, and happy to grind Edgar into second gear for the pleasant, solitary ride to the town dump just beyond First Bush. He felt in command of things. The truck rattled and puffed dust all the way up Front Street. Children stopped to stare like ragamuffin refugees waving with their eyes at the liberating armour.

One wave was for real. A flutter of yellow hanky at the Emma Street intersection. Pretty girls lining the ravaged streets; only their beauty remained as thanks and promise.

'Horace!' Peremptory snap of the hanky, a peach semaphore on the afternoon breeze.

He hit the brakes; the troop-carrier halted at the curbside.

'Miss Sawbush!'

She was just below the driver's window, her face haloed by yellow hair, and perfume. In the afternoon.

'I was about to catch the bus to the City,' she said breathlessly.

'That way,' said the Reeve, 'at the corner of Michigan and — '

'I know where the bus-stop is, you silly man.' She was perched on the running-board, and Nanny Bunch, conspicuous behind her leafy curtain, was getting an eyeful of Miss Sawbush's unsecretarial legs below her raised skirt. 'I'm going to the iode meeting,' she shouted past his left ear, 'to pack food parcels.' This last was delivered so loud that Nanny Bunch winced in her confessional, then smiled ruefully.

'Would you be kind enough, Mr. Reeve, to give me a ride to the City line? Then I won't have to transfer.' Very loud, so every house within the block could attest to the innocence of the request. 'It's for the cause,' she whispered to Horace who was still unable to speak.

'Of course, Miss Sawbush. I'll take you right to the meeting hall,' he heard himself shout.

Gloria skipped around the front of the truck and with a practised ease that discomfited the Reeve even more she flung the cab-door open, caught the step with one dainty foot and cruised to a stop beside him on the seat.

'We mustn't be seen like this, Gloria,' he said.

'We're not!' Her laugh was many-sided.

Her chatter as they drove past the last houses on Front Street and headed towards First Bush — full of gratitude and enthusiasm for the opportunities he had unconditionally bestowed on her — disrupted his pleasant hum, but very quickly replaced it with a different kind of melody. He glanced, when he could, at her peony cheeks. They were aflame with enthusiasm. And very much conditional.

'Well, Gloria, there are times when a man has to stand up for his principles no matter what the town know-it-alls are apt to say. Miss Stoneham simply could not take shorthand. And you yourself are the best to judge how complicated a Reeve's correspondence is.'

'And local organizer for the Party,' she added prettily.

The Reeve had no response to such kindness. Nor to the flutter of her hand across the wheel to touch his.

'There!' Her girlish lilt dropped an octave.

'Eh?' He gripped the wheel like a tank driver.

'Over here, silly.' She had a hold on his right hand and there was no mistaking her intent. She was trying to effect a left turn. 'You know the place; everybody knows it.'

Which was precisely what the Reeve feared.

'But I thought you — '

The tank, with four hands at the helm, crossed the road and aimed itself at the rough track at the edge of the Bush.

'What about the iode?' The vehicle lumbered into a grotto hidden from the road by hawthorn and Manitoba maple.

'They're safely married,' said Gloria with both blood-red peonies.

'The food parcels — '

They stopped with a sigh of iron and rubber, all six tires embedded in a carpet of phlox.

'The home-guard has to eat, too.'

There was no mistaking Miss Sawbush's imperial intentions.

'You poor dear man. Working these fingers to the bone day after day. Taking the burdens of the whole town on your big shoulders. Living with a woman who has no appreciation for the man's heart beating so selflessly in this great chest...'

She was giving an illustrated talk, the Reeve discovered, and what solace was not wrung by the voice was delivered with Miss Sawbush's stem-strong, delicate fingers. She was tracing the map of his own desire.

'Not here, not here,' he murmured against her lips that were

typing messages in code across his face and neck. He hadn't even shaved this morning!

'Here and now. Here and now. It's what you deserve.'

'Oh, Miss Sawbush ...'

'Oh, Horace, my darling. My bruised, handsome darling.'

'Oh, Gloria.'

He found his hands roaming her hair, the musk of her long, inexplicably revealed neck. My God, her breasts seemed to be freeing themselves, coming of their own accord into the light, into the shape of his burdened, deserving hands. Oh Quince, they are so soft, so voluntary. What the callouses of the warrior require. You will come to understand this. I promise. King David in his shivering age called for the virgins to preserve the last of his warmth, and they appeared with God's blessing and his wives' consent. It has been designed. You will see that, Quince.

Gloria's legs somehow liberated themselves. They were gripping him in the eldest design. Both lovers contended for mutual justice, searching one another on this rough soldier's bed. Her teeth left pica-marks on his shoulders. She was struggling with his braces.

'Oh damn! Damn. Oh my God!' Her body twitched but not with passion. One of Gloria's gorgeous unmentionable parts had struck the dump-lever behind her.

The grinding release of iron stopped them both. In the silence of their inheld breath they heard a gathering sexual sound as of flesh sliding on flesh. One hundred and sixty-two bags — a week's hoarding of carefully packed, tinless garbage — slid, then tumbled onto the bed of shocked phlox.

In the Manitoba maple a starling coughed — like a sniper.

* * *

THAT, AS IT TURNED OUT, had been their first and last physical encounter. The village simply did not provide a trysting place for chary adulterers. And so during the interminable winter months they must be content with lover's glances at the Council meetings over the Fire Hall. Once he had walked her home because of the trial blackout, but both Misses

Robertson were perched on their verandah, owl-eyes fastened on him. And once Gloria had slipped a perfumed hanky in the Council Minutes and he had sat in his furnace room for almost an hour before tossing it on the coals and watching it burn like the cindrous wings of an oriental moth.

* * *

'MY THAT'S A LOVELY SMELL coming up the register,' remarked Quince through the pins in her teeth.

'Ahh ... I put some wood on,' said the Reeve.

'You must do that again.'

No, not again. They had to be so careful. All in good time, his mother's voice whispered.

Yes, all in good time.

Chapter

12

'you heard about Guy Gibson, Mrs. R.?'

'Just a little,' replied the grocer's wife without dropping a comma in her ledger.

'Got the whole story,' beamed Mrs. Jones, 'straight from Rose Underhill who was over there the saft. Seems they don't want a lot of visitors,' she added, pausing either for dramatic effect or a slight adjustment of her false teeth.

'It's nice to have some good news for a change,' she continued.

'Yes, isn't it?' Four plus seven is eleven, one to carry.

'You won't believe what actually happened.'

For a moment it appeared that Mrs. Redmond was not about to believe, but she finished her column and looked up appreciatively.

'Well, then, here it is ...'

* * *

'BIGGEST SCREW-UP since Dunkirk, that's what I say,' said Charlie Brighton to Maxie Wise.

'That bad, eh?' said Maxie, who already knew the true story but felt it never hurt to get more than one angle on a tall tale.

'Damn right. Got it straight from the Underhill kid, the older one who plays right wing. Seems Guy was hit with a grenade — '

'I thought it was a shell.'

Charlie looked panicky for a second but carried on bravely.

'Got him in the left leg.'

'I see.'

'Blew it right off, at the hip.' Charlie scanned the face of his listener.

'That so?'

'Knocked him clean into kookoo country. When he woke up, he found some locals had stripped him clean. Watch, rings, even his gold teeth!'

Now that was news!

'Yep, hard to believe, I know. But we was in the First One, eh? We know what can happen over there.'

Maxie knew.

'Took all his clothes, too. Except his pants, of course, 'cause they was kind of blown apart. And naturally his dog-tag.'

'Naturally.'

'Well it seems the whole operation was a grade-a screw-up. Units busted up and split apart. Guy gets himself found by a Yankee outfit. They take him to a medico place. Guy can't remember his ass from centre ice, eh; he's got... ah ... magnesia.'

Maxie let it go, for the sake of the art.

'Don't even know his name. That don't stop them doctors none. They just saw his leg off.'

'At the hip.'

'Yessir. Otherwise, he's okay, see. The shell just got the lower half of him. One leg gone, the other bunged up by shrapnel. Well, the missus, as you know, gets her telegram saying Guy's missing and all. Six weeks.'

'I know.'

'Still, he don't remember whether he's a Yank or a Limey or what. He goes to England. Some bits and pieces come back. He thinks he's Canadian. The head-doctors ask him things like what's the capital and when he says Toronto they know he's one of us. So that's where they send him.'

'I'll bet the Prime Minister was surprised.'

Charlie sensed import in that remark but let it slide.

'Then two days ago, it all comes back. Funny, ain't it, how your brains could shut off all of a sudden, like that, and then just switch on again?'

Maxie did not find it funny in the least.

'Well, sir, it did. Clicked on like a toaster. And here he is only two hundred miles from home, and feeling quite chipper. So he decides to surprise the family. Some soldiers drive him down to the Reunion Station, say they'll see him home safe. And, get this Maxie — '

Maxie did.

'He sends a wire, from the station, just before the train leaves' He began to chuckle into his catarrh. 'Figured it'd get there about the same time as he did! Same old Guy, eh?'

Maxie could find no response.

'And I hear they ain't been out of that bedroom since!' His laugh threatened to choke the denouement.

'Now ain't that the goddamnedest true story you ever heard?'

Except for four or five minor variants, Maxie did find it exactly so.

'No wonder we fucked up Dieppe!' Charlie said.

No wonder at all.

Chapter

13

THE WEATHER WAS STILL HOLDING. The sunlight, after so much cloud and snow, was dazzling as if created anew out of some pure prism in the eye of the universe. It put a perpetual squint on the ordinary faces of the villagers going about their ordinary business on a Wednesday afternoon. They tilted their heads, seeing the familiar evolve and stun. Light on the snow transformed their shabby, war-deprived dwellings into glinting pyramids. It drew the symmetry out of shaved roads, clarity from the cartographer's original dream, beauty from the local fancy, harmony from the fortuitous grace of God's Lake, River, abiding plain. Light, locked in the zero of cold, held the village intact. Time drifted in its perpetual presence.

* * *

THE REEVE, sweating and shivering, flung the last shovelful of snow against the high bank at the side of Miss Jeremy's cottage. The old girl, over seventy now, had been the most loyal hockey fan this town had ever possessed. In fact she had been cheering the war-time Flyers on so lustily, back in forty-one, that she had tipped herself over the boards and cracked her hip on the ice. Even as she was carried off, he remembered her lifting a wrinkled fist and hollering some unladylike discouragement to the Wanderer who had originally ruffled her ire. Not too many of them left, sighed the Reeve to himself, puffing and resting on his shovel. She wanted so badly to be at the game Friday night that he had arranged to clean her walk clear to the side door so that Duff Gleason could wheel her out and down to the Rink.

Looking at the village's top executive, sweaty in his stained mackinaw and fur cap, it would be hard to imagine that only hours before he had been seated in the office of a former us senator in his second-best suit (Quince had promised to repair the herring-bone for his trip to the City tomorrow) making important decisions about the affairs of state ...

the first thing he noticed was the secretary's hair. Metallic, like a platinum plate hammered upon by a drunken smithy. It rippled and glowed: a mirror for her lengthened lashes, improved cheeks and carmine lips. Her dress, made out of something silvery and rattling, encased her excessive shape like Lancelot's armour. She flashed a long leg and a starlet's smile.

'His Worship will see you now,' she tinkled.

About time. The Reeve had been sitting in his stuffy tweed — trying to find a modest place for his gaze and listening to the sweat trickle in his arm-pits — for almost an hour. He made a note to return the Mayor's compliment as soon as possible.

* * *

'COME IN, COME IN, my good fellow. Hope you haven't been waiting too long.'

The voice came from a bellows somewhere beneath Mayor Bulliant's protruding yellow vest, and jiggled his chain of office.

'It's been too long, hasn't it?' he hollered, pumping the Reeve's hand dry.

The Reeve winced, grimaced and squeezed out a painful smile.

'Yes, indeed, your Worship.'

'Magnus, please,' he chortled. 'Where was it now? At the Am-Can banquet?' His vest bounced with ingratiation.

'I — I don't believe we've met,' said the Reeve, retrieving his finger.

'Then it's high time, isn't it!'

The bellows had found an even heartier key.

* * *

'GOT SOMETHING IN YOUR EYE?' his Worship asked between gulps on his Havana.

The Reeve hadn't, and said so. But the Mayor, draped impressively in blue serge, was sporting a set of cuff-links and a stick-pin studded with diamonds, and every time he gesticulated (bellows and windmill arms perfectly co-ordinated) they flashed into the Reeve's stare like the multiple eyes of a beetle in a nightmare. His features, too, reminded him of an insect: proboscis, horny cheeks, ears like tiny antennae, and lips that looped and swivelled around his teeth like the mouth-parts of a caterpillar chomping blossoms. In desperation the Reeve tried to glance nonchalantly from time to time at some other objects in the room: the ballroom-size Stars and Stripes to his left, the row of photographs to his right (American generals and presidents he blushed at recognizing so readily), or the blinding February sun that outlined the gargantuan frame of the ex-senator like a glossy in a movie-house.

'Got a crick in your neck, old fellow?'

* * *

'YES, YES, THE DETAILS,' the Mayor said with a great wheezing diminuendo that passed for a sigh. He was obviously a man unaccustomed to attending to the trivia of this world. 'I suppose we must. What did you say we were having at the banquet?'

'Steak, your Wor — Magnum.'

'Quite appropriate, I'm sure.'

'Canada Grade-A,' the Reeve felt obliged to add, holding out his cheroot with a gesture he was finally getting right.

'And the wine?'

The Reeve blinked. 'I'm afraid, sir, that the Lodge Hall is not licensed.'

'A mere detail, my good fellow. Just let me know who to call and I'll fix it. No don't apologize — these are matters that are, you might say, within my customary purview.' The caterpillar grinned ambiguously at the visiting leaf.

The Reeve wasn't sure whether purview was a kind of French wine or not, but he had a clear vision of how the village temperance ladies would interpret the word.

'I'm sure we can work something out,' he said, trying to get his cigar going again.

'I know how these things are done, good sir. Just leave them in my hands. Why, when I was in the Senate ...' and the

former legislator was off once more on a long, embellished recounting of those glory-filled days before his recent, less happy metamorphosis.

The Reeve listened with stage-struck awe, and dreamed of wood-panelling, rink-size Union Jacks, perpetually-lit Havanas, and Gloria Sawbush in a platinum peignoir.

* * *

'MAY I SUGGEST, with your recurrance your Worship, that we limit the players to the Intermediate range?'

His Worship, for the only moment in the fifty-minute tutorial, looked dubious. He had little notion of what hockey was — though he assumed it was a kind of winterized baseball — and less of what 'intermediate' portended. But a man who has delivered and suffered through innumerable speeches in the world's most celebrated parliamentary chamber is not easily nonplussed. He may not have known the rules but he certainly knew his game.

'Go on, Horace, go on,' he smiled voraciously, slipping the cherry-wood cigar box across the desk.

'That'll mean, naturally, that we won't have any players over the age of twenty-two. Agreed?' The Mayor's smile was less than concordial. 'Twenty-two?' 'We haven't got many lads left, even at that level, I'm afraid,' said the Reeve. 'Mostly sixteen and seventeen, they are. Our goalie, who's got a deformed leg, is twenty-one.'

His Worship nodded sympathetically.

'Much the same here. We live in patriotic times.'

But yours are conscripted, thought the Reeve, and blushed at his lack of charity.

'I see your point though. It is indeed well-taken. With such young and relatively unskilled players, we would be less than just to allow older, more seasoned veterans to take part.' 'Precisely. That was the feeling of our Council to a T.'

'We must have well-balanced teams. A good match.' 'Precisely.'

'In the interest of friendly competition.'

'Hands across the Bridge.'

'As two great nations coming together on equal terms.'

'Precisely.'

'As Allies linked inseparably in a common cause,' he boomed across the Senate floor.

The notebook in the Reeve's head was ringing with new phrases.

The Mayor sat back, cocooned in leather. His ten fingers lay crosswise on the meadow of his vest, like centipedes.

'Can I arrange a lift for you, Horace?'

'Uh, no sir. I brought my — my own vehicle.'

'Very good, then.' The smile was dismissive, the eyelets turned in on themselves.

'There is one more thing,' the Reeve ventured.

'Oh?'

'My Council, you understand this was not my own idea, but my Councillors thought we should — that is to say, you and I should — arrange to, uh, provide, uh ...' and he paused, glancing sidelong into the kerosene eyes of Teddy Roosevelt.

'No problem, as I assured you, my dear fellow. I will take care of the Bordeaux — let it be a gift from this democracy to your dominion. Do not worry your head about such trivial notions.'

The Reeve had not heard; he had just retrieved his sentence. 'To provide, uh, proof of age.'

A clock, which the Reeve had not previously noticed, ticked. And tocked. The centipede gathered momentum and occupied the desk-top.

'Birth certificates?' His face looked as if it had just received the first cablegram from Pearl Harbour.

'They are a ... difficult bunch of men. I argued against it, naturally. I pointed out the need for trust on both sides. After all, this is a friendly match. Hands aross the water, I said.'

'You were right, my friend and good neighbour. You and I

have set the rules in this sacred office. We shall seal them with a handshake.'

'With a handshake,' agreed the Reeve.

The Reeve felt his hand in the grip of his Worship; the middle finger — gashed by Wollochuk's garbage can — cried out its betrayal in a voice of its own.

Chapter

14

SKINNY MCKEOUGH led the way, Brian and Fred Underhill following. They were in civilian clothes, the Wednesday practice having ended an hour before, and were headed over the Bridge to the 400 Club. Skinny had decided for them: no more sneaking into the smoky back-corners of the Richmond House. If they were going to play big-time, then they would drink big-time.

'It's okay for you two, you're seventeen,' Brian Underhill had pleaded.

'Not so,' said McKeough, 'we're all eighteen when we hit the States, eh?'

Brian grinned, a little.

'Everybody's equal over there. It's a dem-ah-cracy!' McKeough said, mimicking the infamous Michigan 'o' and laughing before Fred got started.

'Yeah, and they let the men and women sit in the same bar,' said Fred when he had stopped chuckling.

'Equal opportunity for all,' said McKeough.

Fred gave a half-snicker, just in case.

'The purr-suit of happiness, if you catch my drift.'

McKeough winked in what he hoped was a lewd manner, and they all laughed.

* * *

THEY WERE ON THE BRIDGE at the exact half-way point in the span, that invisible line where the two countries met in seeming harmony. There was no traffic. The sky was clouding up in the south-west but the view to the north was as yet unimpaired.

McKeough lay down on hs back below the boundary marker and flung his legs apart.

'Any brat made here's gonna be a half-breed!' His laugh was edged with a wildness that stopped Fred from responding for almost three seconds.

'Hey, what a great place to commit hari kari!'

'For Christ sakes, get down from there.'

'Come on Skinny, that's not funny.'

'Wheel What a view!'

And it was. To the north the sky was ice-black, embossed with stars. The milky way lay before them like a necklace of hope, its cosmic arc spanning oceans. They watched its thin glitter falling away to the north-east somewhere close to the magic island they were all fighting for. It was hard to imagine — watching the ancient, recurring ice of the Lake and farther out the placid, onyx eye of open water — that somewhere the alluvial certainties of lineage and season had given way, that the blood of brothers was being claimed before its time.

'I'm the king of the castle, and you're — '

Skinny, who had been standing on the railing above the boundary marker with both hands glued to an overhead crossbar, suddenly let go, teetering on one child's foot. He flung both arms back in a feigned fall. The Underhills caught him just in time, like the Marx brothers.

'I was just kidding,' said McKeough, taking a long breath. 'Jesus Murphy but you gave us a scare.'

'You might have fallen.'

Yes, into the sky, like falling off the garage-roof arms wide, letting the parachute of the air catch you, the grass cradle your adventurous bones!

'Come on, you guys. I'm gonna show you the time of your lives.' His grin was all-inclusive.

* * *

'I TOLD YOU we'd get in,' said McKeough. 'I just says "we're Flyers, here to look the enemy over."' And slipping him one dollar American.

* * *

THEY HAD NEVER been in a cocktail lounge before. The waiter, in a suitcoat, showed no surprise when they ordered draft beer. It was hard to concentrate on the bottled Schlitz in such surroundings. The table-cloths were striped red, white and blue.

'Yankee Union Jacks,' quipped McKeough loud enough for five tables to hear.

And the women. Dozens of predatory and aloof Yankee girls, loosely escorted by nondescript war-time males.

'Christ, these guys are all forty and fat.'

'They stay open till one,' said Brian, happily scandalized.

'This beer tastes like used piss!'

The one escort who did not seem forty nor fat glanced, once, over at McKeough, then with a contemptuous gesture squeezed the left breast of his willing escortee.

The Underhills looked down at their Union Jack.

* * *

SKINNY MISSED HIS BROTHER. It was as simple as that. Their old man ran the Fish Hatchery and drove the town's only four- door Packard sedan. That is, whenever he was in town. Before the War he was preoccupied with the business, and when he was at home, he spent his time with Skip, coaching him in math and hoping beyond hope that his eldest son would soon tire of hockey and take up school. After all, Skip would take over the Hatchery some day and a young fellow needed more education these days than he had ever been able to stomach. Skip was nineteen when he gave up hockey — for the army. And though Skinny was twice as good at math, and was one of only three village boys over sixteen to go down to the City Collegiate, he got little fatherly coaching. The senior McKeough was off to Ottawa to work on some secret project for the cause (torpedo fish?), returning every other weekend — when he spent his time boasting of how much he couldn't tell about his contributions to the Victory. Or calming his mother's constant fears for her son's safety. Once, when Skinny was collecting his father's suits for the cleaners, he noticed a strange powder on one of the lapels, and his Dad gave him a curious pleading look. It was the closest thing to a meaningful exchange they had had. He had not allowed his father to hear his crying, later, in the loneliness of his room.

But it was Skip who mattered. At first, from England, the letters came every week, some to him alone — newsy and full of brotherly confidences. The girls in England appreciated soldiers; the beer was masculine, the whisky adulterous. To Skinny, it seemed as if he were coming of age through his brother's exploits as he relived them here two thousand miles away. In another year, if it didn't end, he would be there himself, released from math and the tantalizing half-reality of words on a page.

Then, the postmarks changed: Sicily and strange Italian hamlets. Still, the letters came, dutifully, once a month. They were no shorter, mind you, but the handwriting became larger and larger, as if there were spaces he did not wish to fill. They were like ominous silences in a conversation full of knowledge not to be told. Then a two-month gap. His mother in a state of barely repressed hysteria. She would not budge, for hours, from her chair by the window, dreading the sound of every car that might have been a taxi. After a four- week absence, his father came home. He heard them in the bedroom, each trying to muffle the other's rage, then his mother's sobbing going on and on till he wanted to do something desperate. But Nanny Bunch, good soul, arrived with the mail. Two letters from Skip. He tore his open in the sanctuary of his room, not giving a sweet damn about the turmoil downstairs.

As usual, two pages. But one sentence on each. The letters were the bold, shaky, brutal, half-formed scrawl of a child:

January 25,1945
Somewhere in Belgium

Dear Charles:
I am still your brother
Be a hockey-player, we need you
Love,
Skip

Below, his mother was weeping with relief.

He heard his father tell Nanny that the War would be over by June.

* * *

'WHERE THE HELL would this war be without the Marines? Tell me that!'

'It'd be over,' snapped McKeough.

Audrey Whats-her-name with the satin blouse and mobile chest giggled appreciation.

'Over your ass with a toothbrush!'

Fred snickered, dangerously.

The beer was flowing, used or not. Audrey was sipping not-so-gingerly on something she called Doo-bon-ette. The seven of them — three of the Port Rangers who hadn't seen the near side of twenty for some years, the three intruders, and Audrey — had been at it for almost two hours. The Americans, attracted no doubt by Skinny McKeough's bayonet wit, had joined them, and together they had reworked the campaigns of both World Wars along with a fine sprinkling of past nhl heroics tossed in for analogy or relief.

Audrey was sandwiched between her putative escort, the big defenseman referred to only as Lance, and Skinny, who was becoming convinced more and more with each round that she was not totally loyal to the Marines. Her left shoulder and left hip spent a good deal of the time on his side of the blue-line.

'I knew a Marine once,' Audrey ventured.

'In the Biblical sense?' said McKeough.

'Don't talk dirty!' But no blush appeared on this seasoned rose.

'You guys don't even have a Marines,' Lance said, desperate to get back any ground he had lost.

'Yah,' said the pimply one called Tex. 'You guys are owned by the English. You ain't even got a flag!'

'Or generals,' piped up Beau, the one with the drawl. 'Where's your great Canadian generals, huh? Where's your Pattons and Bradleys and Mac Arthurs? You Canucks spent the war kissing Monty's arse-end.'

'Which is a lot smarter than his front-end,' said Tex. Children. Mere boys playing my-dad's-gotta-bigger-car- than yours, McKeough thought, chug-a-lugging his Schlitz and feeling Audrey's very adult flesh against his thigh. And look at Underhill, gawping at her chest like a drooling kid with his first girlie-mag in hand. Well, he was above all this. Let them play their games.

'Ever heard of McNaughton?' chirped an Underhill.

'Yeah, he got fired, didn't he?'

'Let's sing!' Audrey chimed, off-key.

* * *

Clang, clang, clang went his trolley
Dink, dink, dink went her bell!

Boozy harmonics. Everyone singing lustfully. Hands across the International Bridge. Miss us a perched like an unsteady eaglet on McKeough's lap. I should've worn my jock strap!

* * *

There's a long, long trail a-winding
Into the land of my dreams

Old folks, in the far comer with darker memories.

Dance with the dolly
With the hole in her panty
She borrowed from her aunty
In a seaside shanty
Dance by the light of the moooooon!

Young folk, in the centre of the room with more immediate dreams.

Audrey finally had McKeough under wing. Fully.

* * *

BUOYED BY THE BEER, the Underhill brothers had decided to take up the cause abandoned by their commandant.

'And whose army got stuck on the beaches at Normandy, eh?'

'And whose army got their balls kicked in at Dieppe?'

'I suppose you Yanks call Pearl Harbour a victory?'

'And who won the First War? Tell me that!'

Lance's thrust-and-parry was losing some of its coherence as he tried to keep at least one eye on Audrey whose mother- hen instincts were compelling her to peck at the back of Chanticleer's ear.

'We did! We did!' yelled young Brian. 'My Dad fought over there for four years and no Yankee yellowneck is gonna say we didn't win it!'

'Oh, ho, ho! The little chickling has a temper.'

'And I got fists, too.'

'Give Audrey a kissee, lover. Audrey likes big, strong hockey players.' She didn't wait for a reply, and McKeough found himself enveloped by flesh, perfume and a set of mobilized lips.

'I don't fight babies.'

Brian's fist shot across the table and gave a vicious crack to the cheek of an unmanned beer bottle.

'Jumping Jesus!'

'Serves you right, you little twerp.'

McKeough, coming up for oxygen, had heard enough. 'If

you're so goddam tough, Mr. Yanky Doodle, why ain't you in uniform? Got flat feet or a highway stripe down the middle of your back!'

'We'll see who's yellow in this room,' Lance bellowed, clearing the table of bottles and glasses with a wild sweep of his left hand. His right was already coiled.

'Oooooo,' cooed the eaglet, 'a fight!'

McKeough came right across the table, spilling Audrey sideways, and caught Lance with a solid surprise to the forehead. The American went backwards, following his chair to the floor. McKeough was on top of him and for several minutes they grappled foolishly like under-rehearsed wrestlers. Their respective seconds held the crowd back except for

Audrey who hovered over them like a pullet at a cockfight.

'Get the bastard!'

'Kill the Canuck!'

'Watch it, Skinny, watch his right!'

Audrey oohed and aahed as the clinching fighters struggled silently in front of her and she seemed less interested in the outcome than in the excitement of the battle itself. Even the bouncer watched passively, sweat bubbling on his forehead. National reputations were at stake.

The combatants were apart for the first time. Each swung wildly and missed, circling and glaring and raising fur in an awesome display of outraged manhood.

Be a hockey player, we need you. Skinny McKeough swung from somewhere deep within himself and felt the pain as his fist caught the Yankee Lance-corporal square on the jaw. He was staggered, eyes glazed, and he sat down as if someone had pulled his chair out from behind him. McKeough moved in for the kill, bouncing a partial blow off Lance's temple and toppling him backwards. I'll strangle the hugger! As he leaned across to grasp the open throat, he saw the knee start to raise in a purely reflex action.

'Ow! Jesusjesusjesus!' A land mine had just splintered between his legs. The shock crippled him instantly. Both hands went to the maimed parts and he felt himself waddling in ludicrous pain-induced circles.

The laughter was also instant and prolonged. The bouncer's sweat jumped. The Rangers gave a Texas cheer. The old folks smiled melodically. The floored champion, resurrecting some of his dignity, rose to a knee and grinned through blood, holding his hands up in a Phyrric gesture of triumph. And over all the clamour: a girlish trumpet that held in its sustained bleat all the sexuality a proud nation could wish for

.

IT WAS SNOWING. All at once.

'I'm okay, you guys, I can walk. Let go.'

The Under-twins were having a tough time juggling their solicitude and the laughter trapped in the back of their throats.

'You guys saw it, eh? I flattened that Yank, didn't I? Geez, what a story! And then the bastard kneed me in the balls.' Exultation smoothing out the rippling pain. 'Just like a Yank. No wonder they lost Pearl Harbour. But you guys saw it all, eh?'

They had just sneaked past the Customs Building and were now safely on the first lap of the Bridge. Snow everywhere. Finally, the Underhills could no longer contain themselves. They fell into the cozy snow and let their laughter work its way out through their helpless limbs.

'What the hell's so funny?'

'We can't help it, Skinny, honest.'

'What in hell's so funny, Fred Underhill? You want to get what that Yankee got?'

'It's okay, pal, we won't ever tell, will we Brian?' He was still wrestling with some minor tremours.

'Never. Honest, Skinny. Cross my heart.' He was hopping like a little kid in front of the outhouse door.

'Won't tell what?'

Brian looked at Fred, who spoke. 'It wasn't Lance who got you. It was Audrey.'

'Yeah, she made a perfect drop-kick with the point of her high-heeled shoe!'

'Right in the egg basket!'

'Hey you guys,' said Brian. 'I gotta pee.'

* * *

THEY WERE AT THE HIGH POINT of the Bridge. In the numbing cold they had overlapped hands in a solemn vow, sealing their brotherhood. Skinny limped to the railing and tried to see through the snow whose whiteness was as blinding as the deepest blackout; tried to see out over the Lake, the miles of muskeg and eons of ocean to a small village somewhere in Belgium. Fred and Brian held his shoulders as lightly as they dare.

Yes, it would be like falling off the garage-roof cradled in snow.

Chapter

15

MELVIN REDMOND had always been a grocer. As a boy before the Great War he had uncrated oranges, bunched radishes and stocked shelves in this very store. And swept up many a night after closing when Horrie Macintosh and Gubsy Mitchell were out shagging flies in the vacant lot. The tang of citrus fruit, sawdust, green onions, butterwood, his father's apron — these had been breathed in, lifelong. Surely she would have realized that by now. If she ever would. If people ever got their just deserts in this sinkhole of a world. Redmond's Grocery. That sign had stood above the door, occasionally retouched with the original green, for — how many years? Well, since 1880 when the Point was incorporated, when his Dad had arrived from the London dockside with only a belt- buckle to his name. That would be, what? Fifty-five, no sixty-five years. Damn, why couldn't he add? Miss Cartwright had tried, back then, but she had thrown up the chalk and declared him hopeless. But never had the good, stern teacher humiliated him in front of the others. Not like that one standing like Queen Tut behind the cash register, pencil stuck like a stiletto on her right ear (it always dropped off his whenever he bent down or reared back to give his hearty greeting to a customer, clattering on the floor or puncturing a tomato). She would flip open so-and-so's account book at the new page, write out the order as fast as Mrs. So-and-so could talk, spin out the figures at the right, have them totalled and rung into the register, and still not miss a nod in the one-way flow of gossip. Then, 'Melvin, bring up a bushel of potatoes, will you, dear? And open up that new crate of melons — we want the Missus to have the freshest, don't we?'

My God, did she not know what humiliation she wreaked upon him? Day after day. She knew damn well he could not cope behind the register. Not everybody was a whiz at figures. But it was his store. His father's store. Together they had built up this business, with three-quarters of the village now on their list in spite of that foreigner DeVries who had the gall to buy out old man Turnbull and turn it into a groceteria! Service, that's how it's done. Fifty-five unbroken years of service; not arithmetic. Free delivery. With the horse and cart before the War; he, a boasting lad of eleven behind old Dolly, covering every cobble in the village. And sometimes twice a day when the railroad hotels were still booming. Then by truck. His idea, the year after his father passed on. The first delivery truck in town, and still the only one. The new Ford half-ton in thirty-three. She wouldn't go near it. Not even for a drive in the country after Church. 'It's too noisy, Melvin,' or 'I won't go traipsing about the area in a smelly old truck with that godawful sign on the side!'

Service, not ciphering. A smile tailored to each customer. A chin-rub for the urchins after their licorice. Her highness wanted to get rid of the ice-cream freezer just because Merri- man set up a fancy soda parlour down the street. The little ones still came in, loyal souls, for the extra scoop (doled out when the Queen of Sheba wasn't peeping) and the tousle he gave them or the private joke: hello, general, how's your brother Kernel Com today ? They always laughed. You could count on it. She never cracked a smile, though the old ladies always stayed on and on with their yakety-yakking. Couldn't they tell she wasn't interested? Scribbling away at her order sheet or numbering invoices or writing cheques or filing ration stamps while they droned on contented with her mechanical nod or periodic 'uh huh'!

She was a sour one all right. Thank God for his own cheeriness — there wouldn't be a business otherwise. No wonder either that he slipped down to the storeroom for a recuperative snort now and then. Or kept his Dad's silver flask under the front seat of Wee Bessie. At one o'clock he would be free of her, and all this, as he hit the open road with the afternoon deliveries. And he'd be damned if he got back here by four o'clock to help her with that shipment of canned peas. A little sweat might just make her a bit more grateful.

'Melvin, dear, will you please hurry up with Mrs. Taylor's potatoes.'

Nobody, nobody called him Melvin!

'Yes, love.'

* * *

The old gray mare
She ain't what she used to be
Ain't what she used to be
Ain't what she used to be
Many long years agooooo

He was singing it aloud though no sound passed his lips. The busybodies around town would think he was nuts. Not that he gave a damn. But he really liked it better this way, the great basso pummelling away inside, the organ accompaniment channelling up through the stomach-walls to the belfry in his head. The Walker's Special Old sprayed against his throat like Selzer-water. Good for the lungs.

She might be an old mare but she wasn't gray nor past her prime. She was fire-truck red and her eight cylinders clicked over like an athlete's heart. What a fuss Margaret had thrown when he painted her name, freehand (her signature) on both sides just back of the door: Wee Bessie. And below with arithmetical precision the tiny letters: Redmond Grocery, 31 Front Street, the Point. They hadn't been for a Sunday drive since. Sometimes when he could bear her indifference no longer, he went on his own — to spite her.

The basso sprayed his million-dollar throat once again, and cranked up the organ.

* * *

'YES, INDEED, Mrs. McClarty, it's been a long winter. I suffer from a touch of the rheumatism myself.'

'I've tried everything, Red. Dr. Williamson, from the City, gave me these yellow pills last December, but they're as weak as Mrs. Underhill's tea.' She giggled, her mildewed, bluish eyes lighting up for a moment through her pain. 'I gave them to the canary.'

'Stopped his singing, I bet.'

'Gave him the jaundice,' she tittered, setting her purple hair ajar.

'Ah, my dear lady, you are so brave. You laugh through your suffering.'

'And you, my little teddy bear, are so kind.'
She laced his tea with the rum.

* * *

MARGARET WAS A COLD FISH. A blunt but truthful comparison. Not at first. Though it got harder and harder to recall the first months of their married life, he could never be unfair enough to forget their youthful passion. What encounters on that old bed of his parents in the apartment over the store! She was a foot taller than he and had twenty pounds on him — even then — but he had taken her like a true man. She in turn had given him solace, in her accepting flesh, for the loss of his father. But no child came, except that one, and so he asked her, as consolation, to help out in the store, though, mind you, there was no need. Clerks could be found a dime a dozen after the crash of twenty-nine. Sure it was getting more difficult to get people to pay their bills, but after all the Depression hit everybody hard. And these people were his friends. Very soon after that, the coldness grew between them.

In thirty-three he had taken the money from his uncle and bought Wee Bessie.

* * *

'NO THANK YOU, my dear Mrs. Craig. I really mustn't. Bessie wouldn't like it at all.'

'Now don't go pretending you're bashful on me, Red Redmond. I've known you since you were a tad. Besides, I made it myself.'

No question about that. Her gooseberry wine was thick

enough to do a handstand on. And a couple of cartwheels. He helped himself; his wink was a blind coming down.

'We're all so proud of the Reeve. I nearly swooned when he went on talking so — so elegantly.'

'I was the one who nominated him for councillor back in twenty-five.'

'You didn't!'

'Yes, I must admit to it. I was the first to see his potential. And him so young at the time.'

'Oh, you marvellous darling man.'

'You marvellous, darling girl.'

'Go on now, I'm old enough to be your — your — '

'Elder sister.'

'If I didn't know you better, I'd think you were trying to flatter me.'

'The truth, Peggy dear; we must learn to face the truth.'

'Amen.'

They each turned another cartwheel.

* * *

HE WAS RIGHT. Bessie did not like his drinking. She was beginning to slur just slightly, grazing the lines in the Reeve's lovingly shaped snowbanks along Bridge Street. What the hell, he wasn't running for office! He gunned the engine.

* * *

'oh how i'd like to see that game, Mr. Redmond.'

'And why not? A young thing like you!'

The wrinkles squeezed into a dozen miniature smiles. 'You mustn't tease me. My heart, you know.'

'Strong as a sump-pump, Miss Jeremy. Strong as a sump-pump in a cloud-burst.'

They shared her medicine, and Mr. Redmond wheeled her over to the bay window so she could look out to the Bridge strung like a crystalline net over the River in the crisp, clear air.

'Yes, I'd like to see our boys do it once again. I was there, you know, back in thirty-nine when our boys went up to Landsend and lost it in the final game. Oh, so close. But what a thrill that was.'

'And I remember that as well, dear Miss Jeremy. I led the cheers for the great Bill Underhill.'

'And Skip McKeough. What a goal that was!'

'And I shared in the suffering on the long bus-ride home.'

'And then, of course, I fell.'

'You poor, brave soul. To be so uncomplaining all these four long years.'

Her wrinkled hand, still bearing the grace of her faded beauty, reached over and touched his against the steel of the wheel-chair.

For a moment the Bridge held their private thoughts in its glacial web, the wide world beyond.

'You have a beautiful soul, Red.'

Time for Miss Jeremy's medicine.

never before had Bessie been so obstinate. He would not have thought her behaviour possible. But she parked herself in a snowbank outside Mrs. Taylor's house and refused to budge. He felt like swearing at her, he really did. But that would only aggravate her. 'Come on, old girl, we've been through a lot together. Don't start playing the housewife now. Red still loves you.' There. Sweet-talk will do it every time. Damn! She'd deliberately backed into Parker's garbage cans. What in hell were they doing out on the street anyway? Monday was garbage-day, not Wednesday. 'It's not your fault, Bess, nobody's blaming you.'

He waved at the Reeve, who had stopped to stare, shovel in hand.

But Margaret did blame him. For the store, for the unpaid accounts, for being driven to drink, for her own coldness in bed, yes, even for the child that God took three days after He'd let it be. They hadn't even had time to love it, or miss it, or give it its grandfather's name. After that he began to lose all hope. He found it a strain to keep up his natural cheerfulness. Charlie Brighton, six months overdue on his account, went over to the Groceteria.

He left Bessie in the Taylor drive, and walked across the street to the Underhills.

'the governor-general! Can you imagine that, Red? What a man that Reeve is. And he's coming straight here, not even stopping in the City.'

'When all's said and done, Rose, this village is as important a place as any in the country. Our boys are fighting, too.'

She poured him a second cup of clear tea.

'And a four-star general.'

'Five-star. Yes, I've followed his career through the desert with great interest.'

'I didn't know you took such an interest in the campaigns.' 'Strictly amateur, I assure you.'

'But then you were at Wipers with Will. I shouldn't have forgotten that. You were a genuine hero.'

He let some of the tea slip down the wrong chute, and coughed inelegantly. He needed a little pick-me-up badly. Either his eyes were spinning or the tulips on the wallpaper were. But Mrs. Underhill was death against. He should have come here first.

'None of us will ever forget it,' he said.

'Is the tea too strong?'

'Just right. You make the best in town.'

Rose came close to a blush.

'Have you heard from Bill?'

'Why yes, how sweet of you to ask.'

'Would that be the letter there on the sewing machine?'

'Why, yes.' She always left it in the same place.

'Would you be kind enough to read it to me?'

'But you're a busy man. You've got a store to run.'

He took a draught of the best tea. And she began.

* * *

WHY SHE NEVER even showed the slightest feeling for her brother, the one she used to call, when they were first married, 'the dearest soul I have in the world, next to you.' Right now her Michael was somewhere in Belgium with the rest of the village boys and men — maybe close to the very spot where he himself had — And she said nothing, absolutely nothing. Every week she would open his letter (sometimes right in the store where a customer might come strolling in) and cast her calculator eyes up and down the page — once — then leave it on the counter. For any Tom, Dick or Harry to gawk at! He gathered them all up and kept them in a box under the bed. Scant thanks he'd get for that.

She was a cold mackerel all right, he thought, rubbing his hand over Bessie's still-warm flesh, and catching Mrs. Taylor's anxious wave from the window.

* * *

SILVER THREADS among the gold!

Warbled Mrs. Taylor, her milk-glass fingers threading the keys warily. Then she turned to reveal her vulnerable throat and acknowledge, with a dip of dainty chin, her admirer's applause.

'Pure gold, unadulterous gold!'

They touched goblets of white wine, mutual smiles, and speechless fingertips. The lilies in the silver candelabra rendered assent.

'Just one more, my sweet singing bird, my allouette.'

'A sad one?'

'Yes.'

'I have been so sad, this week. You can't know.'

'Oh, but I can, my dear sad lark. We have been sad together.'

The lark rose from the sweetgrass of its summer fallow.

Keep the home fires burning
Till your hearts are yearning
Keep the home fires burning
Till the boys come home.

Its eyes swelled with the weight of the world's sorrow.

'My dear sad boy will never come home.'

'How you have suffered.'

'Is there no solace?'

'It is a sad, sad world.'

'I need consolation, my dear Red; can the world give nothing but pain?'

Standing behind her he saw his hands idle over her satined shoulder to tremble against the shivering bird-flesh below. She arched backwards and closed her long-lashed eyes. 'Harold?' she whispered, 'Harold!'

'My darling, Bess,' was her lover's reply.

They consoled one another. All afternoon.

* * *

SOMEWHERE IN BELGIUM. 1916. He was eighteen, and going into his first action. Already he had seen enough in the reserve line, waiting his turn. It was spring, and no leaves, no green thing to remind him of any other being than his own, beating frantically within. The smoke-haze met the lowering cloud half-way. One day the sun appeared, orange and simmering. The thumping of Jerry's big guns was exchanged for the shriek of their own just behind them.

He swallowed his rum-ration, then felt his bowel clench. He ran for the open latrine, just in time. Turned to look at his own effluence. The pit was full, though dug last night. The reeking offal, still steamy from the heat of human bodies, seemed to writhe, shimmer, breathe, like a sea of homeless maggots — ugly beyond comprehension. But living, being ...

The guns were pounding so heavily he could no longer feel his own breathing against their annihilating rhythm. He was moving forward, sprawling in the mud — slimy with old blood, rain and faeces — like a crazed hunchback. He was scared and beyond scaring. He was eight years old and lost in an open field on his uncle's farm — space everywhere but no direction; he was screaming his aunt's name but the thunder cracked it and the lightning was aimed at his heart. He dropped beside Tom, his friend of two days. Bullets sizzled into the mud around them. They couldn't go on. But Tom got up and ran forward. He started to follow when Tom jumped back as if he had stepped on a snake. His body unbuckled, came undone. It landed on its side, left elbow stuck in the slime like a wedge keeping the body dry. Nothing moved.

Not even a twitch. Still half-way to his own feet, he watched the wet patch along Tom's crotch widen; little puffs of steam rose out of it into the cold, and faded. The face was gone; bubbling in a helmet.

He was running. And probably screaming. Running back or away, and trying to hold Tom's face in his mind. Tripping over corpses and shell-holes and rifles upright in the ooze. Suddenly his body was lifted straight up into the air and flattened vertically. Pain lit: a hundred bees all over him. A grenade. That was that. He was dead. The last thing he saw was Tom's face — with maggot eyes.

He was found an hour later when the rest of the group had finally worked their way that far along towards the enemy trench. He had run into the German rolls of barbed wire at full speed, the impact tossing him upward and impaling him three feet off the ground like a butterfly on a grid of pins. The Allied shelling had been so severe that the entire section of the German line, not more than thirty yards beyond, had been blown to pieces, leaving no one to deliver his death-blow. One of these shells had exploded nearby, its shrapnel catching the lower part of his legs. That, besides the cuts from the barbed wire, was the only damage.

He was decorated for bravery in London, and sent home. A hero.

* * *

AFTER A BRIEF but violent skirmish, he persuaded Bessie to come out of the hedge and take them both home. It was dark. Almost six o'clock.

Give me land lots of land
Under starry skies above
Don't fence me in!

He whisked out his throat and started in on the second verse.

* * *

SHE WASN'T IN THE KITCHEN when he came up the back stairs. Surely she heard the truck come in. Not that she ever ranted and roared at him; that wasn't her style. She gave him the silent treatment, the old freeze-out. But she liked to do it in the same room, usually waiting to eat her supper with him just so she could out-silence him across the table. Tonight, the table wasn't even set.

He walked unsteadily through the hall to the first bedroom. Not there. The bed was unmade. He tottered over to it. Little dizzy there. Must be getting a cold. He felt very very tired. All those deliveries! And the rural route tomorrow. Where was she? He needed his supper and someone to hold the ice-pack on his head or merely sit and be silent. Damn her. He heard a sound. From the bathroom? Maybe. With great effort and a sense of heroic self-sacrifice, he got up and navigated along the darkened hall towards the bathroom at the far end. It was Margaret's voice all right. But who could she be talking to? His hand accidentally struck the light switch. Jesus, that hurts. What further indignities? As his eyes adjusted to the light he saw something on the hall table beside the phone. Yellow. Telegram. 'We regret to inform you that Corporal Michael Clarke ...' Killed in action. Just like that. He was numb. He stood for a long time, his head a-buzz with memory. He was drunk.

Sobbing. It was sobbing. She was sitting on the back of the toilet, her head almost to her lap, her arms lying senseless against her drawn-up knees, and her whole body was shaking with sobs. A violent hiccoughing sound. He glanced warily across the hall at her, through the open door. He could see she was curled up: a tiny butterfly of a girl.

She looked up, sensing as always his presence. She tried a smile; tears choked it off. Her face was a call for consolation.

But the space between them at that moment was as wide as the world.

Chapter

16

THE REEVE WAS CALMING his nerves with a glass of forty-proof pacifier. Normally he drank a beer or two with Maxie Wise — at home. Never in the Richmond house. He didn't fully approve of the goings-on in that place, but he found it especially embarrassing to sit and watch the town's chief (and only) law enforcement officer imbibing with the best of a bad lot. It lowered public morality in general, he thought. In the old days he used to fall off the wagon once in a while on one of the famous bus-rides to and from a hockey game, after which he suffered the remorse of a daylong headache. In his youth (so distant now) he had, it is true, looked at his face in the bottom of many a whisky glass; he had sown his barley, so to speak, and planted the man.

Tonight he needed just a wee snort to take the edge off his nerves. The fifth of Seagrams VO, a Christmas gift from the Party, had sat unmolested in the cupboard for almost two months. He looked deeply into the half-bottle in front of him for comfort and revelation.

It had been an up and down week. On the up side: the surprise reincarnation of Guy Gibson (though no one had seen him yet except to wave at him through the front window); a most successful visit to Mayor Bulliant of the Port, where he had negotiated in the great tradition of all the past Canadian treaty-makers; Wednesday night's snowfall had been violent but brief, leaving only two new inches of snow which had served to whiten the natural beauty of the village and cover up the fresh dog-dirt (why couldn't those people toilet-train their creatures?) and which he and Edgar had been able to clear away in a brisk three-hour workout this morning; finally, he had cast eyes upon Gloria Sawbush, after his luncheon in the City — driving past in a sable limousine with her distinguished father and a gaunt, official-looking young man who was no doubt one of his lackies; he waved but she was too dedicated to Party business to have noticed him. Well, it was better to keep the whole affair sub roseate for the time being.

On the down side: a mashed finger which was still stinging and threatened the pleasure he anticipated in gripping the hands of vice-royalty and lesser dignitaries; and of course the afternoon's visit with MacAdorey.

He gave another long pull at his soother. The panic was easing. Or was it merely aftershock? Actually in the sober light of his own kitchen, what he had done seemed simple, even inevitable. It had the ring of predestination in it.

Quince at long last had got around to mending the pocket of his herring-bone suitcoat and so he had certainly appeared presentable (dare he say masterly?). He had seen very little of her lately, and was beginning to feel neglected. Had she sensed anything? Surely not. He prided himself on his discreetness, his ability to mask his feelings under pressure. But dammit, did she have to spend every waking hour on the war effort: knitting socks, sticking ration-stamps every Sunday afternoon with Margaret Redmond, organizing the tin collection for him, and visiting the veteran's ward of City Hospital? Didn't she realize that the War would be over by June? What in hell would they do with all those boatloads of oversize socks? Well, perhaps it was better this way: drifting slowly away from one another; they would part friends. He would never say an unkind word about her. Never. She had been true in her own limited country way. But new times demanded a new breed of woman. Could anyone help it if the world grew young while some grew old? It was nobody's fault. Not even God's.

He had not known what he was going to say to MacAdorey even as the cab drew him into the driveway of the mansion on the Lambton Road. He would have to fall back on his instincts. And he did. He lied.

William Dougall MacAdorey did not waste time. Two brandies and half a cigar were all that was needed to clear up the details of the semi-royal visit. The Governor-General was anxious to lay his royal presence upon some of the smaller, yeoman communities of the land before making state visits to his subjects in the cities. The Opposition Party in Ottawa was permitted to select one village from each province to be blessed; MacAdorey and Sawbush had twisted a few forearms to get the Point nominated; London was to be merely an overnight rest-stop for the royal train. His Excellency would motor from his private coach on the cn siding in the City directly to the Monument in the Point, where he would give a brief speech to the assembled loyalists, shake hands with the platform guests, and lay a wreath to the dead of two wars. Afterwards the Reeve and one guest would return with the entourage to the Royal Coach to toast the King.

MacAdorey, having outlined the quid, set his brandy down with two fingers, looked the Reeve in the eye and asked him point-blank about the pro quo. Without batting a lash the Reeve lied. He said with a sang-froid that chilled him afterwards that he had in a very circumspect manner broached the issue of 'consolidation' at the village meeting, that its reception had been highly mixed, but with a few more discreet meetings and the patriotic fervour to be generated by a walloping of the Americans on Friday night and a greeting from His Excellency on Saturday morning, he could assure Mr. MacAdorey that he could deliver the referendum vote by July. Especially if the War were over by then.

MacAdorey shook his left hand vigorously, chatted briefly about life in the inner sanctum, and led the Reeve, arm clapped around his shoulder as if he were clinging to the Stanley Cup, to the side door.

'The future belongs to men like you, Macintosh,' he said.

'The twentieth century belongs to Canada,' quipped the mla-to-be like a man of the world.

* * *

SO SMOOTH. He had told a simple lie as if God, not the Devil, had prompted him. Why then did he feel such a black panic at the pit of his spleen? Half a quart of whisky had not tamed his rebellious nerves. What on earth could go wrong at this stage? The game was on; coach Duncan had the boys primed; there would be wine with the steaks (root-beer for the cautious). The royal visitation was assured. The streets were as neat as if he had used a razor to shave them; the weather was holding clear and cold; Gloria would be waiting in the belvedere for her lancelot, and it would be she joining him for the royal ride. Together they would make their exit from this burg and enter the future on the other side.

The whisky glass shook in his hand.

He needed some fresh air.

Chapter

17

'HEY, YOU BUGGERS, take it easy. This is only a practice!'

The fatherly voice of coach Duncan dispensing advice to the village scions.

'Let's hope they're as nasty tomorrow night,' soothed Doc Jenkins, easing a band-aid on the gash over the eye of Bummer MacDonald.

'Ow! Take it easy.'

'It's gonna be a lot tougher out there against the Yanks,' said Doc (the honour was self-inflicted), wiping the blood on his sleeve.

Skinny McKeough had just been cross-checked into the far comer by one of the second-string defencemen. Skinny was normally the smooth-skating playmaker on the young Flyers' club, staying out of corners and letting his booming shot do most of the talking for him. But tonight, under the three-dozen bulbs strung across the open-air Rink, he had rumbled and bulled his way through the scrimmage like a driverless tank, spilling 'opponents' into every trench and shell-hole of the toy battlefield.

Finally, Lard McGee, the only twenty-two-year-old on the squad, who was neither quick of skate nor nimble of thought, realized he had been speared more than once and drove McKeough into a comer he couldn't escape from. The clash of armour-plate was heard all the way to First Bush. Both combatants fell heavily, the larger landing flush on the smaller.

'Okay, McKeough, we're even up,' puffed Lard, rolling over.

'Even up your ass,' shrieked McKeough.

'Save it for the Yanks, eh! Break it up,' suggested the Coach, sliding towards them.

Skinny did just that. He splintered his stick on McGee's back.

'Hey, you could hurt a guy doin' that!' the big fellow mused, and laughed.

McKeough completed the reconciliation by breaking Lard's nose on his fist.

'Christ!' he yelled, 'You've broken my hand.'

Doc Jenkins arrived with a mop.

Hands across the Bridge.

Chapter

18

MANY IS THE NIGHT that Reeve Macintosh walked the streets of his village, summer and winter. A walk made him feel at home, as if he were retracing in his own steps the random, myriad footfalls of his ancestors. Not literally, though, for he had come to the Point as a young man of sixteen from his birthplace in an insignificant hamlet to the north. But as the Reeve of the people he felt a kinship with them and their lives which stretched back in time more than one hundred years. And when the Reeve felt at home, so did his nerves.

Tonight he felt only out-of-doors, and chilled. As he headed west down Bridge Street towards Michigan Ave, he noticed an archipelago of dark cloud over the Port and the far side of the Lake. Let it snow on the Yanks, not us.

Though it could not have been more than ten o'clock, the village was ominously quiet. Only a sprinkle of lights in the houses along Michigan, hunched against the cold. Everyone was abed, it seemed, getting a deep, satisfying sleep before the unbearable excitement to come. The Reeve felt a little less queasy as he reflected that their heart's-ease was in no small measure due to his own sacrifice. It is the captain who paces the bridge the night before the landing, not the troops.

He turned west onto Front Street, feeling a bit like the

surveyors of old pacing out the lot-lines for a new settlement in the bush. Happy Harry's house was in darkness. What a disgrace! The first warm day this spring he would bring Edgar over here and haul that junk to the Dump, and let the fire have a good feed. Those old ice-boxes and rusted ranges could be boiled down to make one decent-sized tank. Shell-shock or not, some behaviour could be tolerated only so far. He hadn't seen or heard Harry for several days now; strange, because the jibberty-jabber seemed part of the daily street noise. Perhaps he should go in and check. But he wondered what he could say in any event; Harry hadn't talked to anybody but himself since 1916. He passed by.

Flat feet! He would have been the laughing stock of the whole town, a perpetual figure of fun like Duff Gleason or the

Bandit. They had refused to let him serve his King and country because through no fault of his own he had been born with flat feet. What did it matter, then, if he had told a white lie, letting it be broadcast about town that he had a heart murmur. No one was harmed; his reputation survived the holocaust, and he had gone on to expiate his peccadilloes tenfold, serving on the Council for fourteen years and eventually becoming its chief magistrate. A lie — a small one mind you — was often necessary in the affairs of state.

And yet, he hated a lie more than anything in God's world. A man who continually deceived his neighbours ended only in deceiving himself. He believed that, and had tried to build his life and his career on the truth. He believed he had done so. One thing was absolutely certain: he had not deceived himself.

The queasiness returned. Inside he could feel the charcoal wings of a gigantic moth beating panic against the crippling walls.

* * *

WITHOUT PLANNING IT, he had moved north down Fort Street (no one had ever seen a fort or remembered why it was called so) and onto Wellington. His own home lay a block to the east. His feet took him west. To the barn.

It was the last building on Wellington before the vacant lots which separated the village proper from the Pott's Lane settlement. The perfect spot for a lovers' tryst; he was appalled that he had not thought of it sooner. Stan Denfield owned it but lived two blocks distant. The bam was tiny, having been built to house only one animal, and consisted of a stall with a storage bin for oats, and a hay-mow above. Atom lived in the stall, eating his way through the dreary winters, to be resurrected in June in time for the sulky-racing circuit. The Reeve had lost many a two-dollar bet on that gelding at the Dominion Day races in the Point. At the moment he was willing to forgive past betrayals, for the loft above that splendid, incommunicative beast would prove to be their winter grotto.

He was at the stall window peeking in, but what he saw was entirely in his mind: a hay-mow with a sort of manger hollowed out in the middle; two lovers, skin glistening in the moonlight of the tiny upper window, cradled in its surrogate warmth and dreaming spring from the quarter-green of clover and timothy. Below, the gelding breathed out essence of cold, its ears sighing at the lovers' sounds above, its comprehending eyes like holy candles liquid in the moonlight. The beast dreamed, out of time. Snow sifted in like tuneless music. Overhead, the stars beheld.

* * *

GUY GIBSON with half a leg. The black moth stirred in the dark of its own making, uttered a flannel cry. Little wonder he wouldn't leave his house. This war would cripple them all.

With no heed to politics or self-preservation, the Reeve's feet drew him onto Pott's Lane.

* * *

HE WAS STANDING IN FRONT of the Marovitch place. The moon had just gone under the encroaching cloud. The front half of the house sat in darkness, all three floors. From the back section an orange light shimmered on the drifts, warming them. Accordian music: lifting and falling against the night. Voices, in chorus.

As the Reeve moved towards the music, the first snowflake touched the earth.

* * *

'COME IN, come in,' grinned Marovitch. 'We've been expecting you.'

The Reeve was startled by this remark, and not without some apprehension. But something in the old man's voice drew him easily over that profane threshold. Although he pronounced his 'w' like a 'v' and 'you' came out 'choo', there was an earnestness and sincerity about the manner and a pure cadence to the whole sentence that gave it the clarity of perfect English.

The singing had stopped with his knock. The Reeve could see on his first glance that the accordianist was Valdy Wollochuk, flanked by his chorale: Ivan Blinski, Leo Petrov and Alex Kurilski. These he recognized outright. Opposite this group he noted only a blur of Slavic faces, berry-brown, with large receptive eyes. In the unsteady light from the fireplace at the far end, they grinned a welcome at him like a row of walnut dolls. In the middle of the bare room a wooden table, unvarnished, laboured under the weight of a half-dozen vodka bottles and a huge, yellowing half-cheese.

'Come and meet some of my friends,' Marovitch said. 'Gentlemen, this is our Reeve.'

The Reeve put out his left hand.

* * *

MAROVITCH HIMSELF, though strong-boned, was really a small man in his early fifties, the Reeve guessed. The outsize hands seemed foolishly inappropriate to the tightly-muscled frame and they flopped out of control when they landed beside a glass or a chair-rung. This man has not used his hands very often. The Reeve was having difficulty adjusting his notion of the town bootlegger to the face and manners of Nickolai Marovitch. His face could only be described as kindly (if he had been a woman, the Reeve would have suggested 'sweet'), and his manners as aristocratic.

'You like vodka, ya?' said Wollochuk with a ceremonial grin.

The Reeve nodded his approval.

'It good for ulcer!' roared Blinski, and Marovitch slapped his thigh. The Reeve noticed, with a shudder, that the hand was deformed, the fingers squashed together as if someone had taken a sledgehammer to them.

The firelight played shadows against walls and over the exotic, gathering faces, lending to the room an eerie blend of warmth and something slightly sinister.

'Haff another' I said Kurilski, turning towards the fire for the first time. The left side of his skull was caved in like a dent in a bean-can burnished by flame.

How much? the Reeve was about to ask but said instead: 'Yes, thank you.'

'A toast to the Reeve!' cried Marovitch.

They roared some unintelligible but well-meaning gibberish and clinked their glasses. Wollochuk rose, all two hundred pounds of him, and hurled his glass into the fire where it burst like a grenade.

'Please,' the Reeve said, 'go on with your singing.'

'Oh no, no. You are our guest,' said Marovitch. 'We wish to drink and talk with you.'

The Reeve had no reply.

* * *

'DO YOU THINK the country will put the Liberals back in once the War is over?' said Marovitch.

'Well now, that all depends,' ventured the Reeve, looking for words amid his amazement and the vodka haze.

'Mr. King not be King,' said Kurilski, letting his chuckle come to rest in his belly.

'Very true, very true indeed.'

They had all pulled their wooden chairs in a circle around the table, the captain's chair reserved for the chief guest. The cheese looked as if it had been shelled. Marovitch brought out fresh supplies. With the fire behind them and no other light, the Reeve had the feeling he was in a cave. The denizens of the place leaned forward, awaiting the Reeve's pronouncements.

'You yourself have been to Ottawa?' Marovitch prompted.

'Only once, I'm afraid.'

Once was more than enough.

'I myself am in provincial politics.'

'Ah, ya, like Ukraine?'

'A little,' allowed the Reeve. 'But of course the Party has connections in Ottawa.'

This met with universal approval. They toasted the capital.

'And how do you assess the running of the Wartime Prices and Trade Board?' asked Marovitch, refilling the Reeve's glass.

'Well, that is somewhat out of ... ah ... my —purview.' General demurral here.

'However, Bill MacAdorey says ...'

They toasted Bill MacAdorey.

Blinski threw a grenade.

*   *   *

'OUR BOYS vill vin, no?' said Kurilski. 'They haff good team.'

'Our victory is certain,' said the Reeve, skidding on the soft 'c\

'But these are not the Flyers of old, are they? We all remember the great teams of the thirties. I'd give a case of vodka to see Bill Underhill again. My, could that fellow score goals.'

'Good for us to liff near rink, no?' rumbled Blinski.

'Ve beat those Yankees good,' said Petrov.

'And poor Guy, eh? He won't skate any more,' said Marovitch, a look of sadness coming into his eyes deeper than a mere lost limb.

They toasted Guy Gibson. Blinski's eyes brimmed with tears. The Reeve looked at his face in the bottom of the glass.

*   *   *

'the guffenor-cheneral! How you do that?' asked Wollochuk, his fingers tapping out a silent melody on the keyboard.

'Yes, do tell us the whole story.'

'Well, it's a long one, Nick,' demurred the Reeve, glancing hopefully around the table. Kurilski had fallen asleep and was slumped beside Petrov under the table. No one noticed.

'Ve only haff the night.'

The Reeve cleared his throat, pawed at the fog in front of him and began.

when he finished only Blinski and Marovitch remained upright. They gave a boisterous cheer and raised their glasses. The Reeve's glass was a perfect bull's-eye. Blinski, with a thousand shattered glasses ringing in his head, eased himself earthward, his petrified smile disappearing below the table- top.

* * *

'IT'S VERY KIND of you to ask, Horace,' said Marovitch.

The light was ember-thin, a mere glow like a sunset or false dawn. His host had lit a small religious candle on the table. The Reeve could no longer see the walls, shrouded in shadow.

'My daughter Lena is now in Stratford. At the normal school.'

'I see, I see,' murmured the Reeve, sipping on the special brandy Marovitch had just produced.

'We are proud of her,' he continued. 'She is going to be a teacher.'

'Yes, I see, I see,' said the Reeve, skidding and slewing.

A look of despair, of utter desperation flashed in and out of Marovitch's eyes caught in the candleflame. 'As I was,' he said.

The Reeve doused his shame with brandy.

* * *

NEITHER HOST NOR GUEST had spoken for some ten minutes when the knock sounded at the door. The Reeve jerked himself awake.

Marovitch smiled. 'Ahh, that will be our second guest. He is late.'

He returned with a strange figure at his side: a large man who had once kept his body trim with labour but was now running unmistakeably to fat. He was dressed fit-to-kill, the Reeve thought, but his posh double-breasted was strangely out of style. His queerly knotted tie, the narrow drape in his trousers, and the untamed mutton-chop whiskers made him look like a tin-type of one of the Fathers of Confederation.

The eyes, however, completely dominated the face. They were deep and Satanic black.

'We've been expecting you, sir,' said Marovitch with obvious deference.

The Reeve stood up.

'This is Horace Macintosh. Our Reeve.'

'We haven't met formally but I know him well,' said the stranger in a voice as resounding as a preacher's or politician's.

'Horace, this is Cap Dowling.'

* * *

'BUT YOU'RE DEAD. You died a broken man in 1888,' said the amazed Reeve, recalling his knowledge of local political history.

'You are correct,' said Dowling, not at all amazed. 'I lie in the village cemetery, unwept for.'

The fire had gone out yet the room seemed suffused with a half-light from no visible point of emanation.

'You were the first Reeve. Right after incorporation.'

'You know your history. At least the insignificant parts,' he said cryptically.

Marovitch had disappeared. A chill pervaded the room, not the bracing air of the winter-night, but a damp, numbing cold as of caves or tombs.

'Where's Marovitch?' snapped the Reeve. His initial anxiety was giving way to anger and extreme irritation.

'I am your host now.'

'Like hell you are!'

'An apt epithet,' commented the new host.

'I'm leaving!'

'Go ahead, I'm not here to stop you.'

The Reeve's body hugged its chair.

'You were the one who sold us out to the railroads!' he shouted, gaining the offensive.

'Yes, but there are many ways of betraying a trust.'

'Just what do you mean by that?' retorted the Reeve too quickly.

'Do you wish to see?'

'There's nothing you can show me that I don't already know.'

They moved together towards the door.

* * *

WHERE WERE THEY? What in sam-hell was going on? He had expected the full blast of the snow to chill him to the bone when they stepped outside, coatless, into the night. But it was warm, balmy as a spring evening. He felt grass under his feet and smelled lilacs. A bat bounced on the dark overhead.

'I'm going home,' announced the Reeve.

But he didn't.

* * *

THEY WERE WALKING through a dense bush in an area where he was sure the tracks had been as long as anyone could remember. Cap Dowling said nothing, striding in front of him and not checking to see if his guest was following. After twenty minutes they emerged into a clearing. Before them lay the familiar Lake with the river-mouth to the south. Bridgeless as it had been when he was young. But where the lighthouse had stood for seventy years, his eye discerned in the moonlight a weird shape. A sort of palisade made of cedar- posts jammed into the ground, forming a half-circle with water behind. In the middle of the circle he could just make out what appeared to be bark houses.

'Where are we?'

'You are an historian, I believe,' said Dowling. 'Do you not recognize the place?'

'Of course not.'

'These are houses, and the people sleeping in them were the first visitors to this place.'

'Savages?'

'Indian peoples. Attawandarons. We burnt them out.'

'We?'

'All of us.'

'You're mad! That was a long time ago. They battled among themselves. I read my history book in school. We took this place and we civilized it. We made farms out of this useless bush. We-'

'Yes, we did. You have made my point. Do you know where they are now?'

'I tell you, I don't give a damn. That's water under the bridge.'

'Come.'

The stranger's suit had somehow swum together so that it

looked more like a soutane. His figure had slimmed down, and his face was a gaunt shell encasing two self-igniting eyes that pierced the Reeve like crucifixes.

* * *

'IT'S A PLOUGHED FIELD.' Before them, in the dunes near the beach, lay a plot of land about the size of a cornfield which had been ploughed irregularly into mounds surrounded by the first crop of spring weeds.

'This was their burial ground. Sacred earth to rot the flesh and sustain the spirit through the infinite wheeling of time.'

'Was?'

'Yes.'

At last the Reeve saw. In 1925, his first year on Council, they had unanimously decided to let the City Yacht Club excavate the Slip and build a marina, on this very spot.

'Enough,' said the Reeve.

'But we've only begun.'

* * *

IT WAS AUTUMN. The evening cleansed and revived. The Reeve knew he was walking along a very familiar street. The shape of these houses was unique, and unforgettable. But this could not be Pott's Lane. These houses were beautiful, fresh brick and white trim with roses in the yard and groomed spirea. They were lit up against the night like the pleasure cruisers still plying the Lakes. Inside he could hear the unlicensed laughter of men and the descant response of libidinous women.

'The railroad hotels?'

'You are learning.'

'But this must be — '

'The 1880's, yes. And the scene of my own treachery.'

'I know.'

'But you don't. You think I was in the pockets of the railroad barons. I wasn't. You think I went along with them and let the City take the railyards and freight business away from us. I didn't. The building of the City tunnel was already planned. No politician could have stopped the inevitable withdrawal of those services. The City was destined to grow around us. To our credit we in the village have held to our own ground. Like the Attawandarons.'

The Reeve had no comment.

'My betrayal was even greater. What no one but you and I know is that a large shipping firm was willing to come in and buy out the railroad property. They were going to expand the freight sheds. They would have kept this street alive.'

'But you — '

'I was Reeve of all the people. But there was a federal seat open in Lands end up the Lake. They too wanted the shipping business. No money passed through my hands. A discreet promise was made. I spoke eloquently in Council against the new venture. I convinced them that the Tunnel would be built here, that we would get the railroads back. I let them know the new outfit was American-owned and exploitive. They believed me because, after all, I belonged to the party of Sir John A. I had inside knowledge.'

'But you didn't get the Landsend seat.'

'I lost the nomination, yes. I did not sell this village out for thirty pieces; that would have been almost venial. What I betrayed was a trust. And I am buried here as I deserve.'

A burst of laughter from the Queen's Hotel, as if someone unknowing in there had just told a whopper of a joke.

* * *

'MORE?'

'The last.'

'What do you want with me? Who sent you? He felt a hand on his arm. Almost fatherly.

* * *

THEY WERE AT THE FOUNDRY, the town's only large industry since the sellout of the eighties. He knew it was 1938 from the automobiles parked near the plant. He detested this place. It belched sulphurous smoke and the banging of iron against resisting iron bruised his ears two blocks away. Across the street from the Foundry lay the City, its five-storey skyscraper fully visible over the fully-leafed trees. The summer air hung over them, saturated with noise and dust. Only the dp's and a few desperate whites could work in that half-acre of Hell.

They seemed to be above the scene with a clear view of the plant and the surrounding streets. To the north-east he could see, half in the Point and half in the City, the squalid shacks of the workers, abuzz with flies and worse. Then he looked south along the City Road.

'What are all those people doing on the other side of the street?'

More than a hundred: unemployed ruffians by the look of them, bulky scruffily-clad young men with ten years of frustration and rage in their eyes, which were, to a man, fixed on the smudged windows of the Foundry opposite. Each hand held a weapon: baseball bat, two-by-four, tire-iron. At either end of this group, he discerned to his amazement thirty or forty uniformed policemen. Even from this distance he knew they represented half the police force of the City.

'Do you remember now?'

'Yes. We had some trouble down here in thirty-eight. But I wasn't here. Quince and I were at her parents' farm. Her father had just — '

'After the fact,' said the host, but did not elaborate.

'What are they going to do with those things?'

'Surely you knew all along?'

'I didn't, I swear it.' An edge of panic in his voice. They were on the ground now, across the road. The curses of the mob were clear and terrifying.

'Scabs! Bohunks! Get your Hunky asses out of our plant!'
'Go back where you belong!'

'In a shithouse.'

'Come on, fellas, let's crack a few skulls!'

The sable moth inside him stretched its wings, beating against the darkness like a baby's hands against the night. His eyes refused to close.

'Why don't they do something?'

'They can't. They're City cops. They can't cross that boundary line. You should know that only too well.'

He was starting to know it better than he wanted to. The strike of thirty-eight. A sit-down really. The first one in Canada. A subversive notion brought in by the big Yankee unions who got it in turn straight from Moscow. None of the whites would go along. They formed a company union, being sensible men. The dps who came to our country on our charity and our mercy displayed their true colours. They joined their commie friends and sat down beside their machines. For two days. The work of the Foundry stopped. The City police refused the Yankee manager's request to remove the illegal sit-downers. Meanwhile their fat women waddled out from their shacks and tossed salami and foul bread through the open windows. The Reeve had seen none of this. But he had heard the wild tales afterwards. And shut both his ears. It was no business of his nor of the Council. The Mounties should have been brought in. That's what everybody said and believed.

'Who's that in front of the Foundry gate?'

'A former friend of yours; look closer.'

'I've seen enough. I beg you.'

The uniformed figure was Tubby Kingston, the village cop before Piersall took over the next year.

'There's nothing he can do. Why don't he get out of there?' 'He was the only man that day with a clear conscience.' 'They're crossing the road!' He watched like a rabbit gluing its eye to the snake's tongue.

With a terrible cry, like men pouring over the trenches for the first time, the mob moved across the street. The City cops stood and stared, uncomprehendingly.

Tubby Kingston shouted something like 'Halt!' but was drowned in the howls and disappeared under a flail of bats. As the men swarmed through the gate, Tubby lay on the sidewalk, blood oozing from his mouth still frozen to its cry.

'It's time to go inside,' said his host quietly.

'No, no, please. I had nothing against those people. You must believe me!'

The sleeves of the host's black robe widened, stretched, and feathered; he waved them like the wings of a prairie vulture.

'Hop on,' he commanded.

* * *

THEY WERE ON THE GLASS roof, staring down at the drama below. The Reeve's eye felt as if it were propped open with needles. He had not blinked in an hour.

'Look upon your work; weep if you have any heart.'

The goons had gained quick entry; no guards blocked their path. The workers — weary, hungry and scared — sat beside the machines they had loved and cursed for more than a decade. The goons seemed even more infuriated by this lack of resistance. They swung their weapons blindly, breaking them on the backs and the raised arms of their victims. They worked in utter silence broken only by grunts of pain, moans in the aftermath, and the unforgettable sound of wood on fleshy bone. For several minutes not a worker moved, as if they could not bring themselves to the realization that this was actually happening.

'Stop! In the name of Christ, please stop!' screamed the Reeve. No one heard.

Blood and oil ran together. The thudding echoed eerily through the cavernous foundry.

'No! No! That's — that's — '

Kurilski: the lead pipe catching him on the left side of the head, knocking him to his knees. Like a sledge on a pumpkin. Get back, Marovitch! Get away! Nickolai Marovitch moved in front of his friend in time to stop the death-blow with his raised hand. He began dragging the unconscious Kurilski towards the exit at the rear.

The Reeve was sobbing and shouting simultaneously. For a blissful minute his eyes closed. When they opened again he could see the workers running, dragging their wounded with them and screaming in Ukrainian or Polish their rage and humiliation. One man, hounded by goons to the rooftop, dashed past the Reeve to the edge. The Reeve watched, powerless, as the crazed man leaped to the tarmac below. He lay still, his back broken, unattended.

'My God! My God! This didn't happen here. Not here.' 'We must see the last,' his host whispered, not unkindly. 'Not here!' sobbed the Reeve, hands over his eyes.

* * *

THEY WERE JUST ABOVE the trees that ringed the northeast side of the Foundry.

'They're going for the houses!'

They were. They were going to clear out the whole nest of them. The Reeve watched in his helpless anguish as the goons pursued the workers to the doorsteps of their pitiful shacks. Women and children, shrieking in dismay, dashed out of side doors, clambered through windows and fled like refugees from a blitzkreig.

'They're going to destroy them!'

'Yes, the purging must be complete.'

He saw the first house go up in flames, a matchbox in a holocaust. Several goons found more pleasure in hacking the shanties to pieces with axes and tire-irons. In minutes the entire ghetto was consumed.

'I didn't know, God knows I didn't know!'

* * *

his host was holding him by both shoulders. His suit had rematerialized, and they seemed to be in a room again. A fire flickered behind them, cozily.

Cap Dowling grasped both his hands and stared into his

eyes. His look was half-pity, half-anger, part human and part something else.

'Two days before this tragedy, the day before you went off to the country to be with your bereaved mother-in-law, you sat at the Council table not two blocks from here. A motion was presented by one of your fellows, to wit: that this village Council refuse to waive the by-law forbidding City police to cross City Road to the Foundry. You were the last to vote. Like the others, you voted "yes".'

'Yes, yes I did. But what good would my single vote have done? There were eleven others. Many were older and wiser than me.'

'Reeve Downing was about to retire. Everybody in town knew that.'

But I would, have thrown it all away! The years of service past. The chance to assume leadership, to serve my people better. What good could come from a meaningless gesture of principle? And none of us knew; won't anyone believe that?

But all special pleading was blotted out by the image of Nickolai Marovitch's outstretched, mutilated hand.

* * *

The reeve was alone.

Chapter

19

SNOW: SOUNDLESS, out of the deepest silence we know. Gathering in its immaculate enfolding the cris-de-coeur of the souls it laid its grace upon.

No witness, here or there, to see the thin figure of church-organist/choir director/leader of the Boys' Band as he paced the back alleys of his adopted village. No one saw or heard the three athletic shadows come out of the downfall, and circle their victim.

If they were surprised that he made no move to cover himself they did not say. They went about their business methodically, ritually. No word was exchanged. The prey lay facedown, limbs flung out casually as if in sleep. The slim back, coatless, gave a slight hunch — braced.

No blow came. Instead: one knee on his spine, almost gentle; another on his right arm, more insistent. He jumped as if jolted by a cattle prod, but the knees held him. A black boot dropped past his terrified gaze and found its mark. The cry came from his whole body, stood upright in his throat. It had gazelle's eyes.

Something in the snow flinched at the breaking of bones.

The shadows of the three whitened and were gone.

Chapter

20

MRS. TAYLOR, unconsollable in black, left her house at precisely 9:00 a.m. of a Friday morning. The word of Margaret Redmond's telegram had seeped, overnight, through the cisterns of the village.

Against the snow's alabaster foliage, she was a sable nun seeking out news of the dead. Her shawl spread outward as she strode like the carbonous wings of a crow.

Chapter

21

THE BOYS AT MAXIE'S were taking bets.

'We'll just have to go with the score,' sighed Maxie.

'Not a soul in town'll bet a brown nickel on the Rangers,' said Harry Bridges, the baker.

'They like their sheckles too much,' piped Grogan, the Bandit, who had fought in the Boer War and had a stump to prove it.

'Well, there's no way our kids are gonna lose,' said Charlie Brighton. 'And that's God's truth.' He spoke like the old soldier he was, having seen both earth and the other place.

'It's a matter of loyalty when you get right down to it,' said Merriman, who had cheered from the sidelines in two wars and knew what it meant to keep the home-front strong and brave.

'I'll take five to one; for the Flyers, natch,' said Duff Gleason.

'It'll have to be a pool,' said Maxie, gently. 'I'll get the numbers set up and we'll draw.'

'And if the Rangers win?'

'No way those Yanks are gonna come over here and take our game away from us,' said Merriman. 'It's just about time those cocky bastards got taken down a peg.' He spilled his Pepsi.

'I'll commit hari kari in Grogan's shithouse if they do!'

offered Duff, the patch of Yankee soda-pop spreading across his pants-front.

'And I'll — I'll sue you for polluting!' squeaked the Bandit.

'We'll win; for King and country,' said Harry.

'Providing, of course,' said Maxie in his slow way, 'the Reeve is able to keep those guys from cheating.'

That stopped the flow of Pepsi for a full second.

'Overage players,' explained Maxie. 'The Reeve's got them to agree this is an Intermediate game. No one over twenty- two.'

'But who's gonna check their teeth, eh?' quipped the Bandit, showing all of his toothless grin and waving his stump perilously close to his Orange Crush.

'That's what I mean. More or less.'

'We gotta trust our Reeve. That's what it comes down to.' 'Damn right. Here's to the Reeve!'

Five Pepsis and an Orange Crush rose as one: for King, country, and Reeve.

* * *

NO CLICK OF CUE AND BALL accompanied this man-talk. The poolroom behind the smoke shop where they were gathered around the Quebec heater lay in semi-darkness. Not like the days before the War when snooker-sharks like Snuffy O'Toole came down regularly from the City to challenge the local talent like Skip McKeough and slim Bill Underhill. The side-betting was brisk and boastful. Wins and losses were transformed into legends that lasted for weeks and kept the Pepsi flowing at Maxies and the tumbler's full at the bootlegger's a block away on Pott's Lane.

* * *

144

'SUPPOSE WE CAN get some of them Bohunks in shanty-alley to cough up a few bucks for the pool?'

'They're Ukrainians and Poles,' advised Maxie.

'They're all the same anyhow. A dps a dp.'

'And who's to say they're loyal, eh?'

'Yeah, who reads all that mail they get from the enemy? Never know what might be in all that mumbo-jumbo.' 'Spies,' said Duff, then lost his train of thought.

'Most of them have been here longer than us,' explained Maxie with more resignation than patience.

'Won't even show up at the game, I'll bet.'

'Bet they will!'

'Two to one!'

'Even!'

'You're on!'

'Dammit to hell!' yelped Duff. 'Somebody spilled themselves on my pants.'

Chapter

22

THE REEVE WOKE UP. His eyes wouldn't open but he knew he was awake because he could hear a dog barking; the familiar soprano of women's chatter floated up to his ears. He could feel the comforter wrapped snugly around him, though a draft seemed to be toying with his exposed throat. Light flooded the room, washing clear through his reluctant eyelids. The middle finger of his right hand cursed him. His thoughts were these: it's very late, I've slept in; this is Friday, day one of my triumphant exit; the furnace had gone out and I'm freezing to death; the eiderdown has turned to ice; I've just had a Judas of a nightmare.

He rolled over and faced the world. Christ in Purgatory! he was outside. He flung out his arms and snow scattered like feathers in all directions. Not quite outside. He was sprawled on his back in the doorway of his rear verandah, the door ajar, both objects held fast by a three-foot drift. He couldn't see his feet, nor feel them. Little wonder the nightmare had galloped unfettered through his head this past night. Frost-bite, he thought with a sigh; my legs are gone. They'll have to wheel me up to the podium, like Roosevelt.

He tried to sit up but his head spun like a yo-yo that couldn't quite make it round the world, and he fell back, striking his head on the step. I'll never drink again, Quince, I promise. He let the pain from the hangover and the stabbing where he'd struck wood run freely through him; it was no less than he deserved. But a leader without legs? Well, he wouldn't have flat feet at least. He thought of poor Guy and dear Miss Jeremy in her crippled age. Could Gloria love half a man?

It must have snowed all night. At least six inches on the side fence. The streets! Obliterated. No vice-regal entourage could get through it. He must clear the streets. He must. He was the Reeve, they were counting on him. He lurched up and to his amazement stood on his feet, dizzy but upright. They were alive: pain stabbed straight up from his toes to the pit of his stomach with icicle-teeth. He tried to cry out but his jaws were sealed with cold. Tears squirted on his cheeks, warming them. His blood rushed excruciatingly skinward. In his mind, he fainted.

I must clear the streets. He took a step towards the plough buried to the hubcaps in the driveway. My God! He felt as if both feet had been blown off and he was walking on the shattered stumps of his ankles. He glanced back, looking for blood on the snow. He fell into the fence. Black butterflies with maimed wings flapped before his eyes. He got up, his stumps ablaze. His left elbow went numb. Broken, no doubt.

Edgar was waiting for him with customary patience. With some difficulty he opened the cab-door, frozen shut, and hauled out the crank. The drifts in the drive were two feet deep, and it took him several minutes to work his way to the grill, his swollen right hand against the hood pushing him forward like an oar. He waited until the dark wings settled somewhat, then inserted the crank. He couldn't grip it with his right hand. He switched to his left. Solid grip, but the cracked elbow refused to cooperate. Damn! Would he have to use his teeth?

The handle flipped over, driving the pain deep into his shoulder. Again. Edgar cleared his throat. Again. Edgar wheezed. Again. Sweat and tears scalding his face. Come on, Edgar, I can't do this again, I can't. But he did: Edgar chortled and shook the snow off his coat.

It's going to be a good day, thought the Reeve.

* * *

THE HEAT FROM THE ENGINE soon thawed out his legs and feet (not without some disquiet on the part of their owner) and by combining what strength remained in his left hand and his right arm he was managing to steer the plough with minimum discomfort.

He roared up and down Michigan Ave, the street which led to the City and the Bridge, spraying snow like wheat from a thresher. Mrs. Jones and Mrs. Underhill, on their way to Redmond's, were left speechless on a corner. Orie Wollochuk, companionless on Bridge Street, barely saved his sled from the manic sweep of the huge blade.

Up and back three times and the street was bare to its hard-packed surface. The plough slowed for the next pass, and like a giant cookie-cutter sculpted a fine edge to the rough embankment. This manoeuvre caused the Reeve to sweat tears as he tried to hold the wheel steady with his improvised grip. The old truck jarred and bucked, but toed the line.

The sun climbed to the frozen noon.

* * *

BY ONE O'CLOCK every street in the village was cleaned and shaved. In the early morning after the squall, the village had resembled some wilderness settlement, a clutch of haphazard rooftops with nary a pathway between them; the snow had rounded off corners, rumpled gables, confounded architecture. In three desperate hours its Reeve with a surveyor's eye had drawn it back into the twentieth century.

Edgar was wheezing like a pneumoniae, but more work remained. The King's surrogate and the former us senator would view the town in all its civilized glory — every drive and walkway visible to the hearth!

The brothers Macintosh began.

* * *

FRESH CLOUD had just covered the four o'clock sun when the Reeve turned onto Pott's Lane. Edgar balked like a milk-wagon horse on a strange route. The Reeve, aching from toe to cowlick, urged him forward with a vast patience. For the first time in days he felt a calmness at the centre of his frantic motion. He heard his mother's voice, softly iterant: 'All in good time, my boy, all in good time.'

Edgar got his second wind and together they began ploughing the snow from Marovitch's driveway.

* * *

THE REEVE WAS SOAKED to the bone with his own sweat. He was finished except for Kurilski's and Grogan's at the deadend. Ten minutes more. His shirt was stuck to his back; he had forgotten to take off his tie. Then with a sigh as deep as the Void itself, he realized he had been wearing his herringbone suit since the meeting with MacAdorey yesterday afternoon. It reeked and fermented even as he collapsed against the wheel, the soul washed out of him. Second-best tweed — for an almost-king! For a second he wondered whose side God was really on.

A tap on glass cut through his reverie. He looked up to see Alex Kurilski smiling and waving at him, the burnished dent in his left temple clearly visible.

He waved back, thinking a smile.

* * *

HE WAS HALFWAY to completing Kurilski's driveway when he noticed that idiot Grogan stumping through the snow towards his outhouse, chattering to himself (boasting no doubt) and flapping his half-arm like an insane semaphore. Every nerve in the Reeve's right hand crackled in its own kindling. He let out the clutch without a thought to Edgar's fatigue, and gouged Kurilski's drive bare with a single thrust. Something within him stretched and snapped. He plunged the accelerator to the floor, ground into second gear and veered towards the Grogan place. The rheumy-eyed old braggart would just have his pants down and his boorish bum poised for the bomb-drop! He'd scare the lying poop right out of him.

With his bombardier's eye the Reeve sighted his missile so that it would shave snow within an inch of the outhouse. Edgar leapt to the challenge. They sprayed flak all the way down the left side of Grogan's driveway. He'd think the Boor grenadiers had landed on him! However, at the moment of contact the Reeve's wounded hand betrayed him: went numb to the elbow. Edgar, as surprised as anyone, bounced sideways. To the left.

Before the jolt tossed his head against the windshield, the

Reeve heard the crunching mesh of steel and brittle wood, and a wild shriek that might have been his own.

* * *

THE REEVE BLINKED. How long had he been unconscious? The old man, that blood-welding cry of terror? He tried to open the cab-door but it wouldn't budge. Only then did he realize he was sitting at a forty-five degree angle. He scrambled up to the passenger door and leapt out, striking his forehead on the frame. Dazed and waist deep in snow, he flung his limbs in every direction, half-running/half- swimming around to the driver's side. An awesome scene awaited him.

Edgar had veered left, catching the outhouse square on the backside and burying himself in the ten-foot drifted bank around the spot where the shanty had stood. Rotten lumber lay scattered to the north and west. The main section seemed to have sunk or been driven completely into the drift itself. And the old man with it. If he were not dead from the impact, then surely he was smothering somewhere beneath the crushed snow and ruptured timber.

The Reeve had rescued only one person in his life before now: he had pulled Little Guy Gibson from the waters of the Slip after the boy had fallen off the dock. But he knew what to do. As he had done before, he tore off his coat, suit-jacket, trousers and shoes, and dove head-first into the water. And as in that previous episode, he sank through the drifts out of sight like a sugar-cube through iced tea.

* * *

KURILSKI WAS THE FIRST of the unemployables to arrive on the scene. Within seconds he was joined by Marovitch, Wollochuk, Petrov and Blinski. Down the freshly-ploughed street distant figures from the poolroom appeared, running.

'Dropped like a stone,' explained Marovitch.

'He committed hari kari,' suggested Duff looking about, bewildered.

At that moment they were joined by Grogan who had come over from the place in the field where he had been 'taking a leak' ('Why mess up the outhouse,' he was to comment many times later at Maxie's or wherever more than two cronies happened to be gathered).

'The Reeve jammed a nut or something?' he said. 'That outhouse is more than thirty years old.'

'Was,' said Duff.

'A regular hair-loom, it was.'

'Come on, fellas, we better dig him out,' said Maxie. Marovitch and Kurilski had just returned with an armful of shovels.

'I'm gonna sue!'

* * *

THEY DUG DESPERATELY in total silence for five minutes, heaving up splinters and yellowish-looking lumps of snow. By which time half the town had assembled around the scene of the tragedy to give much-needed advice or exchange hushed predictions.

'What's the world coming to?' reflected Grogan, sensing an audience. 'Seems a fella can't take a peaceful crap in this town.'

One of the shovels struck something resilient. A toe: waving?

'He's alive!' Communal cry of joy and relief.

In a minute, with seven shovels working ever so carefully, they uncovered both legs of the precious artefact kicking like a baby's for life.

'Watch the elbow!'

'There's a shoulder!'

'Okay, boys, grab a leg and we'll pull him out.'

A curious smell began, at this point, to pervade the odour-free winter air.

They pulled. The Reeve of all the people, before the marvelling gaze of most of his people, came up with a squish and a pop!

He turned himself upright, disdaining the helpful hands

around him. Everyone drew back simultaneously as if struck with a wave of mustard gas.

The Reeve, covered head to toe in some yellowish semiliquid, rubbed his eyes and mouth clear of the noxious substance.

'Shit,' he said by way of explanation.

Chapter

23

EVERYBODY WAS PRESENT. From his lofty position on the bleachers at centre ice (especially erected for the occasion) the Reeve surveyed his fiefdom. Directly across from him — standing behind the boards, perched on snowbanks or jittery on makeshift benches — were the home-town fans. The women and fatherless children were gathered to the left from the red-line all the way to the shanty which housed the teams — he could see at a single sweep the Misses Robertson; the mistresses Underhill, Jones, Thorpe, Merriman, Bridges, Duncan, Piersall and Wise; the widows Taylor, McClarty and Craig; and Miss Jeremy in her wheel-chair mounted on a platform right at the blue-line. (Somehow Duff Gleason had manoeuvred her here without serious mishap through he had managed to run over his dunce-cap twice.) And barely visible among such a throng, the shy countenance of Quince herself.

Quince had asked him nothing about his nightmarish adventures, accepting with infuriating trust his story of having fallen asleep in the truck. Indeed, she seemed solicitous to a fault over his escapade at Grogan's, peeling off his fouled underwear, dressing his hand, forehead and elbow, soaking him in a warm tub for an hour, and then rubbing down his entire body with horse liniment till the aches became almost bearable.

154

For a moment he thought he detected a certain sensuousness to her rough touch, a deliberate lingering over the stretched thigh muscles. She spooned hot soup and tapioca into his starved body, then laid out fresh clothes: a new white shirt and purple tie she had bought as a surprise for him, and his second-best tweed suit straight from the fast- service cleaners in the City. She brushed his fumigated hair till it glowed black and silver. She said almost nothing but the occasional 'Tch, tch' and 'oh dear', but kept giving him odd sideways glances when she thought he wasn't looking. She kissed him on the forehead as he left.

It almost unnerved him.

Almost. He had been to the brink and back these past seven days — through Hell's offal, so to speak — and was not about to throw it all away because of one woman's wiles during a moment of weakness. The master plot had been set in motion, and if it had not always run smoothly, it was nevertheless pointed to a single, inexorable denouement.

He surveyed the scene to the right. The men of the town and assorted boys and ruffians blotted out his view of the Lake, stretching right around the open end of the Rink to the near corner on his side. The gang from the poolroom formed a subgroup of cheerleaders: Maxie, Charlie Brighton, the Bandit, Merriman, Harry Bridges, Red Redmond and Duff Gleason (capless). And hundreds of others: some in uniform, others showing the bright blue and white colours of the Flyers. And by himself, both arms on the rail, stood Guy Gibson harbouring his own private cheers. Next to him, on a raised dias (clump of snow) in full military dress Chief Piersall stood on guard for King and country.

Along the end boards, unabashed by the poorest seats in the

house, crowded the Pott's Laners, three-deep, with their babushked wives and flocks of round-cheeked offspring. Their broad smiles were praise.

Who, then, was missing? Happy Harry who never came to any civic function (who cared?). Martha Gibson and Little Guy, both undetected on the streets since Tuesday. Strange business, that. And Marg Redmond, of course; in mourning; they all understood. And Cameron Hornby. Even more strange; someone said he had not shown up for Wednesday's practice of the Boys' Band. Would they be ready for the ceremony tomorrow? The Reeve had not had time, given the nature of his day, to find out.

On either side of the bleacher-platform, though he could not see them, were arrayed the American visitors who had arrived with the Ranger team on their sleek silver Greyhound. They were making a considerable noise for their paltry numbers, their miniature Stars and Stripes flapping in the breeze like tiny slaps on the cheek.

And strung across the entire width of the Rink, at the Reeve's request, was a banner proclaiming: hands across the bridge.

The advantage of having the villagers placed opposite was obvious to anyone with the slightest political bent. They had an unobstructed view of their chief magistrate as he sat in his pride at the dead-centre of the Official Party. To his left were his Worship, Mayor Bulliant, and his gaggle of followers — all dolled up in oversize raccoon coats which made them look like polar bears with impetago. His Worship's secretary clutched her master's right paw; her platinum hair, unshielded, tinkled with each wave of cheers that rolled west to east across the Rink.

'Yeah Flyers, yeah, yeah!'

Or, from north to south: 'Ya Flyer, ya, ya!'

The Mayor was exceedingly ebulliant this evening and deferential to a T. When the photographer from The Reporter snapped their picture, the erstwhile senator clapped a hairy arm on the Reeve's good shoulder and smiled down at him, not the camera. Then his Worship directed the startled young man to take a shot of the banner, and went so far as to suggest that its motto might make a fortuitous headline in the Saturday edition.

'Horace, this will be a night to remember,' he quipped.

On the right side of the platform, the Reeve was even happier to note, sat Mayor Goodchild of the City, William Dougall MacAdorey and their entourage, apparelled in respectable black lambswool coats with white silk scarves bunched modestly at the chin. Among them, and seated (to the Reeve's immense delight) between the Mayor and the dignified figure of her father, sat the radiant Gloria Sawbush. Several seats further down, he noticed (to his immense relief) the brittle young man he had seen with her in the City on Thursday. He had not been able to catch her eye thus far, but she had come, and persuaded her father and his people to come along as well. That connection would not be without benefit, he mused, but his real thoughts were drifting towards a midnight loft in the still winter moonlight.

At the moment only the last item of that happy thought was in doubt. Clouds had been building up over the Lake to the north-west since late afternoon.

'Go Rangers, go!'

A pathetic half-chorus soon smothered by the full strophe from the opposite side.

'Go Flyers, go!'

Neither team was going yet because they had not come on to

the ice. It was five minutes to face-off. The Reeve could feel with his all-encompassing sympathy the tensions and frustrations of his people after the long joyless winter at the end of a long and cataclysmic war. Though there were few Catholics among them, the feeling tonight was unmistakeably carnival.

William Dougall MacAdorey tugged at his sleeve. Time for the official ceremonies. The Reeve and the sometime senator delivered ten-minute speeches which were, considering the absence of any collusion, amazingly similar. The applause was equally polite.

'Here come the Flyers!'

The night to remember was under way.

* * *

THE FIRST THING the people of the Point noticed was that the Rangers, resplendent in yellow and black, were half again as large as the Flyers, dashing in their Huron-blue sweaters and snow-white pants. They grow them big over there, was the communal response: must be all that com. Our boys may be small but they're faster: look at them go!

'Yeah McKeough! Yeah, yeah, Skinny McKeough!'

The teams were skating around doing their warm-up. On the second pass the villagers' eyes adjusted to the colour and dazzle, and it was noted with some unease that the yellow sweaters bulged suspiciously with what appeared to be a corpulence abetted by the enthusiastic and legal consumption of beer. By the third go-round the keen of eye detected with considerable puzzlement the presence of a dark and unadolescent stubble on the chin of each of the visitors. And when they began hollering and exchanging vows during the warmup of their goalie, they did so with accents never heard in the State of Michigan.

At about the same instant the Reeve came to a conclusion not dissimilar from his constituents': not one of the Rangers had seen the age of twenty-two for some time! They were without any doubt refugees from the semi-pro leagues of the South. The initial burst of applause for the home-town youngsters dropped ominously to a shocked murmuring.

All eyes turned upon the Reeve, but his eye was cast in the direction of the chief American negotiator at his side. Mayor Bulliant, however, kept his beetle-brows aimed straight ahead like Washington's across the Potomac; he looked as if he had just swallowed the cherry-tree whole.

'Come on Flyers!' yelled the Reeve so loudly his finger hummed.

'Stick it to 'em, you big Lancer!' shrieked a feminine voice straight from the loins, and three of the Flyers turned to stare.

'Face-off,' said the man in the striped shirt.

The battle began.

* * *

AT FIRST, the size and experience of the Rangers proved no match for the speed and heart of the Flyers. Time after time the kid-line of McKeough and the Underhills sped around the outstretched elbows and knees of the American defence and fired freely at the opposition net. But McKeough, the play-maker and marksman, was having difficulty getting any velocity on his shots, due in part to the treachery of his right hand sturdily encased in plaster. In a dozen shots on goal, only Fred Underhill had managed to tip in one of Skinny's looping drives. In the mean time the lance-corporal and his platoon of heavies did manage to corner a few of the speeding blue-shirts who staggered up as if in shell-shock. At the end of the first period, with the Rangers held to just two shots on goal, the Flyers led 1-0.

The villagers, weary of wariness and self-doubt, were ecstatic. Between periods they shouted and sang.

Our country's name is Ca-na-da
Her children proud are weeee

They held hands and danced on the packed snow. From the end-zone came a haunting Ukrainian song charged with joy, tinged with elegy. Silver flasks flickered under the lights. Thermos bottles added fuel to a fiery bliss. Miss Jeremy took her medicine and shouted. Guy Gibson waved his crutch like a baton. Redmond sprayed his tonsils and crooned. The Reeve waved to Gloria and she waved back.

This was better than the War of 1812 and Fenian Raids rolled into one!

The visitors remained silent but unchastened and not without hope. Theirs was a long and embattled history.

Just as the referee dropped the puck for the start of the second period, the snow began.

* * *

NOT A SQUALL as on Wednesday or again Thursday night, but light and continuously falling — the kind children pray for on Christmas Eve. At first it made the villagers more cheery; they dipped a little more deeply into their hot-water bottles and shouted even louder through the muffling snow. This was truly a winter carnival: Canadian style. And what better goat to sacrifice to the approving gods than these ersatz Yankees. At which point, to prove His faithfulness, their common Guide allowed Skinny McKeough, sprawling forward on his smashed wrist, to tap the puck home. 2-0.

'Crush the Yanks! Crush the Yanks!' they chanted.

A group of boys led by Orie Wollochuk played 'Warm Beef' against the boards to the tune of 'Yan-kee' Yan-kee!' Miss Jeremy had to be helped back into her wheel-chair. The Reeve looked heavenward, and smiled. At last. In good time.

* * *

THE SNOW KEPT FALLING. At the ten-minute mark Lance caught a tiring McKeough, playing every other shift, and threw a knee, an elbow and the butt-end of his stick into him. The knee caught his groin (still tender), the elbow his rib-cage and the stick his right cheek. McKeough collapsed in a heap.

'Cross-checking,' yelled the ref with suitable understatement.

'Power play! Power play!'

'Send the bum back to the States!'

'They won't have him!'

McKeough meanwhile struggled to his knees, ignoring the blood running into his mouth and the pain in his lower body. His sights were set on the overage Ranger moving smugly to the penalty box.

'Gotcha again!' shrilled Audrey Whats-her-name over the din.

McKeough may not have heard the remark, but he switched into high gear, streaking cross-ice behind his tormentor. He swung his stick with his last ounce of outrage. The crowd drew in a single breath, waiting for the lethal crack. What they heard as they exhaled through the snowy air was a mild thump and a snap. McKeough's cast came down flush on Lance's shoulder pad; his stick cut open the ice below.

Skinny howled all the way to the dressing-room, Doc Jenkins racing behind.

For a moment no sound was heard but the shush-shushing of the snow on uniforms, ice and overcoats.

'Five minutes for deliberate attempt to injure,' snapped the ref.

Not a partisan could bring himself to disagree.

The Reeve turned heavenward again but all he could see was the relentless, downfalling snow.

* * *

'HE'S ALL RIGHT,' whispered Doc in the Reeve's ear. 'Didn't crack the cast. I'll drive him to City Hospital just in case.' 'Thank God,' breathed the Reeve, and grimaced.

'They've scored,' said MacAdorey.

* * *

THEY HAD. On their power play. The ice, slowed by the inch-thick snow, nullified the speed and quick poke-checking of the Flyers. The Rangers, bringing their brute strength into play, had little difficulty knocking the Flyer defence down in front of the net and controlling the puck at the points.

'Yah-hooo!'

Tex had put the puck in the net. 2-1 for the Flyers.

* * *

THE VISITORS took their turn.

Over hill, over dale
Up and down the dusty trail
Oh those Rangers keep rolling along

The hands on the other side of the Bridge clutched the railings a little more tightly.

'You big bullies!' screamed Miss Jeremy, and had to be pacified.

No need to panic. There's lot of time, thought the Reeve. These people have not weathered the storms I have. Time seasons a man, it —

With one second left in McKeough's penalty the Rangers scored again. Brian Underhill skated to the bench, his nose spraying blood like a flit-can.

The Reeve began to sweat in his tweed.

* * *

BETWEEN PERIODS Duff Gleason and some of the boys cleared two inches of snow from the ice. By the time the players returned the red-line was a blur again.

Some of the male stalwarts of the village were seen slipping off into the snowy dark for some refuelling before the third period began. The women held hands and made ineffectual swats at their restless children. The Reeve tried to clear up some small details with MacAdorey concerning the Governor-General's visit and, while he was turned in that direction, to catch a glimpse of Gloria Sawbush. She was discussing Party business with her father and the young Turk who had just joined them. Off to the right he could hear his Worship giving dictation to his secretary.

Across the ice, Quince waved to him.
The snow's descent was unrelenting.

* * *

YOUNG BUMMER MACDONALD was the next Flyer to be brought down. He limped off with his knee twisted at a strange angle. The home-town crowd was growing wrathful; their premature joy, cut off in mid-refrain, was turned inward, and ugly.

No penalty was assessed.

'Kill the ref!'

'Turncoat!'

'Judas!'

They stopped play to clean the ice again. Ten minutes to go; score tied. But still the puck would not move for the Flyers whose spirits had been dimmed though not extinguished by the continued body-checking of the Rangers. The Americans, with more stamina and the patience which comes with experience in the trenches of the semi-pros, bided their time and used the body with the reckless courage characteristic of their nation.

No one, not even the Reeve of the people, was surprised when the Rangers took the lead at the twelve-minute mark.

From the Halls of Montezuma
To the shores of Canada
We will fight our country's battles ...

There's still time, said the Reeve to anyone who would listen.

* * *

FRED UNDERHILL'S EYE PUFFED SHUT, unable to repel the elbow jammed into it. The kid-line was annihilated.

'Two minutes for tripping,' barked the ref smartly.

The Ukrainians broke into song. From the women's section a burst of hopeful applause — mothers and wives and widows accustomed to cheering from the sidelines. Their men, from a different perspective, hoped but stayed silent.

'We never win a battle but we always win the war!' Grogan: the old guerilla.

* * *

NOT ALWAYS, thought the Reeve watching in dismay as the Flyers failed to get a shot on goal during the power play, and the casualties mounted.

* * *

THE RANGERS SCORED AGAIN at the fifteen-minute mark. The ice was cleared of snow and Yankee flags.

* * *

LARD MCGEE, his nose broken again, had used his body like a sandbag all night. With no one near him he fell to the ice, exhausted. Tex wobbled around the fallen sapper and lifted the puck disdainfully into the upper left corner of the net. The goalie with the deformed foot got up slowly on one leg. Lard crawled through the jubilant Rangers towards the Flyers' bench. The tears streaming down his face were not for his pain. Tex swooped past and spanked him — once — with his stick.

Play was halted till the Rangers stopped laughing.

* * *

WHEN THE RANGERS SCORED their fifth goal, Chief Piersall fell off his dias and had to be cleared from the ice.

* * *

THE FINAL WHISTLE BLEW. Only eight Flyers could still stand on their skates. The score was 11-2.

* * *

DIGNITY, that was the password. We must maintain our dignity at all costs, thought the Reeve. Every ache in his body was renewing acquaintance with his brain, but he stood up tall in the garish, snow-filled light and made his way towards centre-ice for the presentation ceremonies beneath the banner.

'Get your rear off that bench, MacDonald, and get out there!' he hissed, passing the slumped and battered recruits.

Neither of them made it.

* * *

IT WAS CLAIMED AFTERWARDS, in the poolroom and grocery store, that Chief Piersall started the whole shocking affair, but the eruptions which took place on that snowy evening with visibility near zero seemed to occur spontaneously from a number of quarters — as if something communal and poisonous in the body politic had seized control of each citizen at precisely the same moment in time and more or less for the same reason.

But the Reeve, who was no more than three feet away, saw the uniform of the Chief flash by him and hurl the remnants of its dignity headlong into the file of Rangers standing at attention on the blue-line. Unquestionably he heard the thunk of Piersall's skull against the cup that guarded the most precious parts of one lance-corporal. If that was a signal, it was well read.

* * *

THE REEVE WAS TUGGING at Piersall's back with his good hand, Lance's moans filling his ears, when someone hit him from behind with a pack-sack.

'Oooooh — a fight!' shrieked Audrey, swinging her purse and catching William Dougall MacAdorey right where he wore his names. The International Friendship Trophy clattered to the ice and broke in two unequal pieces.

'You bully!' She kicked the Reeve on his right shin.

MacAdorey kicked her back.

'ladies and gentlemen, please. The banquet. The ceremony.'

He was shouting helplessly into that part of the din he could see.

'The ceremony — '

Someone pushed a mushy snowball into his second ceremony.

* * *

ON THE ICE, three Flyers were holding Tex down. Lard sat on his face. Piersall, his head ringing, jerked out his revolver and fired wildly into the air. No sound emerged.

'Halt! in the name of the law!' he yelled.

* * *

the reeve helped Mr. MacAdorey off the ice. Blue and yellow bodies hurtled by them through the haze.

'It's a riot,' he gasped. 'Call the police.'

'It's all right, sir. Everything'll be fine. I'll just get you to your car and then I'll come back and settle this. It's nothing for you to worry about.'

After picking himself and the Party President off the ice and brushing off the latter's coat, the Reeve continued, 'I'll read them the Riot Act.'

'You do that!' snapped MacAdorey and huffed his way through the snow in the general direction of his limousine.

Where was Gloria?

* * *

THE POISON HAD SPREAD. The Reeve was on the east side of the Rink groping his way towards the gate leading back onto the ice. He heard a series of high-pitched screams coming from the other side. The women were into it. A commotion to his right. He veered that way in time to see Duff Gleason and Red Redmond struggling with a large raccoon coat. The raccoon was losing. It toppled backwards into a drift and disappeared, only a glowing cheroot sticking up obscenely through the quicksand.

Redmond stamped it out with his boot.

At the same instant a second raccoon with an albino top came hurtling at Duff Gleason with a banshee wail. They rolled, locked in combat, into a drift and sank from sight. The drift jiggled and was still. Intermittent puffs of steam issued from the breathing hole.

* * *

my god ! it was a full-scale riot. What could he do? Where was Gloria?

'Reeve, thank God you're here,' sobbed Mrs. Jones, bumping into him.

He noticed for the first time that he was limping.

'They're going for the dressing rooms,' she gasped, looking in amazement at the swatch of hair in her left hand.

* * *

THEY WERE ALREADY THERE. As he arrived at the back door, he heard the stove go over with a crash of clinkers and tin. Half-naked bodies brushed by him in the dark. The Rangers in nothing but their jock-straps were skittering towards the silver bus — a posse of men, women and children in hot pursuit.

'Ladies, please,' he begged in desperation, latching onto the nearest vigilante. She bit him on the left thumb.

'Fire!' a voice cried within.

* * *

THE REEVE HAD FOUND the extinguisher at last and was smothering the flames around the bombed-out Quebec heater with a soapy chemical, bathing several bodies at the same time — some still, others continuing to the death. No one noticed.

Outside again, he discovered the snow was coming down even harder. His thumb had swollen into a rigid appendage. He didn't know where he was, but the battle was raging all about him.

'Hands across the Bridge,' he wailed.

* * *

HE LURCHED from scene to scene, pinching himself and expecting at any moment to wake up on his verandah.

In the meantime:

Guy Gibson and Merriman were taking turns spanking another one of the raccoons with a crutch. Guy was hopping about like a one-legged dervish and laughing with some of his former gusto.

Mrs. Taylor had tackled a robust Ranger supporter and was beating him to death with her leather mitt.

'I've got him, Harold! I've got him!' she chanted.

Miss Jeremy, with the aid of the widows McClarty and Craig, had pinned a burly Ranger (Beau?) beneath her wheelchair. 'You brute!' she yelled directly in his ear.

Mrs. McClarty was working out her rheumatism on his exposed backside. Mrs. Craig hurled invective: 'Damn Yankee, go home!'

Grogan, the old scout, tracked Audrey to the outdoor powder room and demobilized her with his stump.

* * *

ACROSS THE WAY, somebody ripped the banner, lengthwise.

* * *

FOR WHAT MUST HAVE BEEN a quarter of an hour the Reeve sat on a snowbank of his own making and thought about absolutely nothing. Having given up all hope of exercising his authority or carrying out his civic responsibility, he had dashed about blindly, turning over slumped, exhausted bodies and peering into their faces. No Gloria Sawbush, anywhere.

His only thought was that she had escaped unharmed from this madhouse. But what haven would she flee to?

* * *

a great cry down by Front Street brought him back into action. A choric shout as if the Christians had just eaten the lions. He limped in that direction in time to see the silver bus — packed to the buzzer-cords with their friends from over the River — pull away from the taunting, jeering, dancing mob surrounding it. Across one side of it, Orie Wollochuk, or some other hapless urchin, had scrawled in charcoal (with much fervour and little learning):

YANKYS FUK!!!

The Greyhound disappeared down Front Street. The crowd was silent but did not move. They heard it turn onto Michigan Ave. No one budged. Ten minutes later, rushed through customs, it appeared on the Bridge above them.

The Reeve noted with a rueful sigh that the snow had stopped. You could see for miles.

When the silver-winged creature passed the beacon-light which marked the boundary of the two nations, the congregation below, as one voice, sent up a cry of triumph that shook the bones of Cap Dowling in the distant cemetery, ruffled the ghosts of the Attawandarons tending the past and future, and might have been heard as far away as Ypres or Dieppe or the forests of the Ardennes.

Chapter

24

CHAOS, PANDEMONIUM. The Valley of the Dry Bones. Images from his Sunday School days with the Reverend Burns simmered in the Reeve's mind and coursed through his tortured body: to the cracked brow, the bruised elbow, the gashed finger, the dented shin, the newly-bitten thumb, the deep ache of every muscle and bone stretched beyond endurance in the futile attempt to inspire civic decorum and political probity. These physical discomforts, however, were miniscule in face of the mental anguish the Reeve was suffering.

The known world was in shambles. No Blitz, no Juggernaut, no Dieppe could have brought such instant catastrophe to a community as the barbarism of the past hour. All was in ruins: his plans, his hopes, his long dream. William Dougall MacAdorey, insulted and bludgeoned, would take his three names back to the City with his limousine, and never return. The Governor-General would be diverted to a hastily- contrived ceremony at the City Monument, then whisked back to his Private Coach for a drink and a snide chuckle or two over the boorish behaviour of certain country bumpkins (wink, wink). Instead of hands across the bridge or tiny town triumphs, the headlines in The Reporter would read pickled pointers perpetrate mayhem (reeve reneges on riot act). And even if, by

172

some miracle, His Excellency did manage to arrive for the ceremony, what villager would dare show his face after the shame of this night? How many could even get themselves out of bed, or hospital, in the morning? And the streets? Five inches of fresh snow perfectly timed to tweak some Satanic sense of humour. They'd need a tank to get through it. Well, let them all shovel their own drives from here on in!

What was even worse than the communal humiliation was the thought that the event would become a permanent part of the village annals; it would rank with the dispossession of the natives, the railroad sellout, the tragedy of the sit-down. His own grave would lie next to Cap Dowling's, and deservedly so.

And to lose like that to the Yankees! To have fallen for the oldest soft-sell as his kind had done so often, without learning. To have to live beside them for ever and ever, and listen to the daily reminders not only of the humbling defeat at their own national game, but of their primitive and childish retaliation for which there was no moral excuse. It was unendurable. Their faltering pride as a people, so tested by the agonies of this war, would bend and break. And what could ever revive it? The War would be won — by Brits and Yanks, as the last one was. What consolation, then, for the widows and the maimed survivors? The town would be a-babble with Happy Harrys! A dozen Grogans would build shithouses on their front lawns and wave their stumps at the gawk-eyed tourists.

I must stop thinking like this; I will go mad.

The Reeve turned on to Wellington Street. The night was cool but not nearly as cold as the day. The sky lay open, the winter stars dancing on their grand proscenium like the twinkle in a comic's eye. The snow underfoot greeted each step lovingly, content to reflect the moon's eccentric glow.

His future in the Party, of course, was already past. A career nipped in second bloom. He could not move forward, could not seize the destiny which was rightfully his, and yet he could not turn back either. A part of his life was over. He had always burned his bridges behind him, so to speak, and he would do so again.

Quince was a good woman. He would never say otherwise. They had had a good life, he would never deny it. Together they had devoted their lives to the public good. To what end? Public repudiation and personal rejection. All their good works blown apart like a pill-box on the Normandy beach.

The Reeve was through with politics. That decision had been taken the moment his ears had been defiled by that atavistic baboon-howl of the village collective beneath the Bridge built to unify two proud nations. The body politic was not worth governing. It may have taken him two wars, a Depression and forty-seven years to learn that lesson, but at least it had been irreversibly apprehended. From this point on he would give up all notions of public duty, self-sacrifice and lifelong humility. No longer would he devote his life to others. No more would he suppress his natural pride. He would never go so far as to boast — he was incapable of that sin — but he certainly intended to take unlicensed pleasure in his accomplishments.

And the pleasures would be gleefully selfish. That decision had been taken as he had sat in the smoky silence of the shanty listening to the last murmurs of the mob slinking back to their empty houses. He would devote the rest of his life to the gratification of his own whims, lead him where they may. He might go back to carpentry, the trade which had drawn him and his brother here so many years ago. He might even give old Edgar a ring-job and contract out his services to the City. Wouldn't that raise some eyebrows around town! / must not be petty. I won't stoop to that.

And pleasures of the flesh, too. The flesh of Gloria Sawbush, white as a halved snow-apple. That's what I'll call her: my little snow-apple.

He stopped. From the moon's position overhead he knew it must be midnight, or later. Her Majesty sailed above him, unimpeded but eternally alone.

The sudden panic in his chest reminded him that, in spite of all the resolute vows he had sworn in the past hour or so, his entire future hung upon a decision which could be taken only by another than himself. If Gloria Sawbush were not waiting for him in the designated place at the appointed hour, the future of Horace Macintosh would end with the stroke of midnight. A whole lifetime — lived with hope and disappointment, collapse and revival, luck and faith, good will and God's grace — had been drawn through the thousands of allotted hours to a single second, to a room no bigger than a coffin.

* * *

THE REEVE STOOD before the barn for a long time. The snow had clothed it with crystalline silence. Its green shutters, polished by moonlight, gave it the appearance of an old-country cottage at rest in the landscape. It harboured its own quiet, at peace with itself. No need for neighbours, it lived within.

The door at the back welcomed the road-weary traveller. The snow gave warning that another had already sought shelter. Boot prints. Tiny. A woman's.

* * *

THE REEVE CLAMPED a hand to his somersaulting heart, and entered.

Darkness, beckoning. A column of moonlight, Grecian-white, slanting from the window above to the manger below. The breathing of sleek animals, awed by shadow. The whisper of hay from distant meadows. A swollen, half-human eye: curious, male, comprehending.

Atom neighed, flinging his huge Pegasus head into the light, and looked, unmistakeably, upward.

* * *

THE REEVE, HIS SKIN TREMBLING, removed his overcoat and stepped to the wooden ladder below the loft. The bam was warm with body-heat, straw and the enfolding snow. He took off his tweed jacket, shivering, letting his own warmth merge with the room's. He set his galoshes by the ladder and took the first long step up.

* * *

SOMETHING TURNED, lazily, in the soft hay, just under the moon's prism. An arm lifted into it, alabaster slim, greeting him.

'My love, you've come,' he said.

'Yes.' A whisper, emitted as freely as her breathing.

* * *

THE REEVE LAY HIS NAKEDNESS against hers, felt the welcome of the blanket beneath them and the caress of the one she drew over them.

She touched each of his wounds with her mouth. Her lips drew the misery from his abused flesh. They startled with their newness. They revived and prolonged. They resurrected the memory of desire. They were young yet remembering.

For hours he lay like King David, drawing sustenance into his age.

* * *

HE SHAPED HER BREASTS with his scarred fingers, marrying pleasure with pain. His practised hands drew her innocence to the brink. They fell over together.

* * *

HE ROSE ABOVE HER like a prince. They cried out in unison at their coming.

* * *

'MY GOD, YOU ARE SO SOFT, so young. And I have waited so long.'

Coming down, she kissed his tears with her stinging lips. Her thighs were a canopy for sorrow and joy.

* * *

THEY LOVED AND SLEPT and loved again. They woke each other with their hands. He dreamed of consolation, she dreamed of love. As the night aged they grew younger, and the world with them. They prevailed.

* * *

AT LAST THEY FELL into the deep sleep of the innocent or the lost.

* * *

THE SUn through the window woke the Reeve with a start. He sat up.

She was still naked, propped on one elbow, studying his face.

'Good morning,' said Quince. 'It's awfully late, but you looked so peaceful, laying there.'

Chapter

25

THE SUN HAD BEEN UP for three hours, supreme in its isolation, the sky around it untrammelled by cloud except for the ominous gray along the western rim. It shone with equal deference upon the ocean-wide Lake, the ice-bound River, the crystal Bridge, the twinned cities of two nations, the dormant snow-fields of the hinterlands beyond, and upon the tiny peninsula which lay like a cotter-pin at the hub of this universe.

The village itself lay wrapped in snow and sleep. The home-fires, unattended, had expired in the dark; no smoke rose from the chimneys of the hundred houses to cheer the morning. No bootprint marred the flawless comforter of snow. Not a single dog had yet made his territorial mark on the seamless landscape.

The first sign of life — a movement only — came unexpectedly from the south, along what might have been a road to the City. A snow-plough: not the scarlet one familiar to the village with a Reeve at the wheel but a powerful, invading creature, military brown, manned by soldiers, their brass buttons flickering. The double-blade sprayed snow in both directions; it flew straight up, then out, like the under-feathers of a mourning-dove. Behind it a road stretched and shone.

Upon which, when the wings settled, could be seen a line of automobiles — black limousines purring and confident. The leading one had a special glow about it, a sheen so glittering it seemed to be covenant with the sun; and from each of its shining front fenders, there fluttered a royal ensign.

* * *

AT THE SAME MOMENT, though no bell summoned from a church belfry, other movements could be detected, random yet somehow coordinating. Miniature bundled figures emerged from a hundred doorways: tentative, testing the chill, dazed without walk or pathway, their footprints marking the way back.

They came from the north, singly, in their need. They walked from the south, in couples, out of necessity. From east and west they strolled, in family groups, wondering. Towards the Monument at the centre of town, the obelisk of anguish past and of hope.

* * *

THE MILITARY PLOUGH had cleared the way for the vice-regal entourage. A perfect square was cut in front of the cenotaph. From the back of the khaki machine, the brisk uniforms drew a platform, raised it with a series of impressive commands, and lavished it with carpets as red as a king's bedchamber. The podium held its Union Jack with appropriate pride.

* * *

OUT OF THE TROUBLED NIGHT, out of the sorrow of war, out of its own history, the village resurrected its hope, and assembled.

* * *

GUY GIBSON STRODE without a crutch, his wife on one arm, a son on the other. They dreamt of renewal.

* * *

MISS JEREMY, PROUD in her sedan-chair, gave commands her batman obeyed.

* * *

THE WIDOW TAYLOR, RESPLENDENT in mourning, paid homage to the long-dead.

* * *

ROSE AND WILL UNDERHILL WALKED with their two boys, and dreamt of a third.

* * *

MRS. JONES DID THE VILLAGE PROUD in her best satin.

* * *

THE THORPES VOWED to renew old loyalties.

* * *

RED REDMOND, HOLDING his wife's hand, marched to a distant tune in his corporal's stripes, his medal garnering light.

Margaret Redmond, all in black, kept her veil raised, her eyes shining with tears.

* * *

MRS. MCCLARTY, FORGETFUL of her rheumatism, warbled like a wild canary. Mrs. Craig, braced with gooseberry, did cartwheels to a soldier's ditty. They dreamed of the good times.

* * *

SKINNY MCKEOUGH KEPT PACE with his father's strides, swinging his cast to the drumbeat within. Mother and sister kept vigil behind.

* * *

OUT OF POTT'S LANE Nickolai Marovitch led his people, dreaming of nations and the wounds that bind them. Orie Wollochuk gripped his father's hand like a staff.

* * *

GROGAN, THE ONE-ARMED BANDIT, paraded with a slightly constipated strut at the front of his invisible regiment. His grin was world-wide.

* * *

HARRY BARTHOLOMEW, ERECT in tunic and brass, sang for humanity.

* * *

CHARLIE BRIGHTON, Maxie Wise, Doc Jenkins, Harry Bridges, Mitch Strong, Michael Piersall — veterans all, the legion of survivors. The Women's Auxilliary at their side dreamed the peace only gods enjoy.

* * *

SUDDENLY THERE WAS MUSIC, a faraway strain as from distant battlegrounds.

In days of yore from Britain's shore
Wolfe the dauntless hero came

From their parade ground at the school-yard, in perfect file, marched the Boys' Band. And at the helm: the imperial figure of Cameron Hornby, his gold baton keeping flawless, left- handed time.

* * *

BEFORE THE MONUMENT, around the flag-draped podium, the village assembled itself to behold the royal presence.

* * *

AND ROYAL IT WAS. Never had a village of the British Empire been so graced with majesty! The Governor-General stood tall on the platform surveying his subjects with monarchical concern, kingly compassion. Those eyes which had borne witness to the agonies of Africa; the humiliation of defeat, the brief glories of triumph; the separate, colossal deaths of a thousand men, loved and prized — looked fully into the face of each man, woman and child, and knew them. The medals and bars of his Field-Marshal's uniform were no camouflage for the heart that gave them meaning.

And what trappings of royal splendour accompanied His Excellency! Upon the platform flanking the vice-regal Emissary they beheld Mayor Goodchild of the City, five of his councillors, their own Maxie Wise and Reverend Budge, half a dozen Parliamentarians, old Menzies in full regalia, William Dougall MacAdorey, Maxwell Sawbush and his lovely daughter, and at her side, his hand folded secretly in hers, a handsome young mandarin on his way up in the world.

At a signal given by Chairman MacAdorey the Boys' Band struck up 'Land of Hope and Glory' and if the winter chill distorted some of the pure sound of the tubas, no one noticed. They were singing too buoyantly to hear. When the anthem ended, a spontaneous applause rose from the gathering. The Field-Marshall smiled. After the Reverend's invocation he moved to the podium and addressed his subjects.

He reminded them of their courage, the need for steadfastness in times of adversity, the importance of the home-guard, the necessity of high morale, the unstinting effort of individuals. He spoke to them of loss and grief and the incredible valour of their husbands, sweethearts and sons, his voice faltering. Then he turned to hope, and talked of the victories in western Europe, and prayed with them for an early end to their common nightmare. He instructed them to think of their country's greatness, of its immeasurable contributions to the Allied cause, of its mighty factories and glorious democracy. He urged them to dwell on the future whose promise for this wide and blessed land was boundless in the sight of God.

When he stepped back, the assembly clapped and cheered till the platform shook in sympathy. And yet in spite of the awe in which they beheld their King's representative and despite the genuine joy they felt in their hearts, there was an unexplainable holding back, a curious reticence to release the full force of their approbation. Some small but vital element in their happiness was missing.

It was time for the laying of the wreath. A hush descended on the crowd, on the houses behind them, on the Lake beyond. Miss Sawbush placed the wreath in His Excellency's hands. As he was about to move forward to the Monument, a commotion erupted at the back of the crowd. The platform guests froze in place.

Applause. At the far edge of the worshippers — scattered, collecting, gaining momentum. If a Governor-General and Field-Marshall were capable of surprise, His Excellency was: he paused and looked with genuine curiosity at the unexpected turn of events.

The crowd was dividing itself into two halves as if the King Himself had appeared without warning and was moving among His people to bless them. From the space between the halves emerged a familiar figure, bathed in applause. The Reeve did not seem to acknowledge it, his eyes intent on the Union Jack in front of him. He stepped up to the platform and made a formal bow to His Excellency who had turned to greet him. The Reeve was seen to whisper some words to the Governor-General. The congregation interrupted their praise to catch the royal response.

His Excellency put out a gloved hand and grasped the Reeve's. Without wincing, the Reeve shook it vigorously.

Everyone in town heard the exchange.

'Welcome to the Point, Your Excellency. We are honoured to have you among us.'

'I am here at the King's pleasure, Mr. Reeve. Will you do me the honour of laying the wreath?'

But the Reeve, to the astonishment of his admirers, turned back towards the crowd. He held out his hand. His wife stepped up to the platform, was introduced to His Excellency, and took her place beside her husband. The crowd cheered without compromise, and the Governor-General smiled approval. So they cheered again.

The Reeve astounded all a second time. He went into the crowd and drew to the platform the Widow Taylor. Without prompting, as if she had rehearsed the action a thousand times, she took the wreath by the right edge and with His Excellency holding the other side they moved to the Monument and placed upon its base the symbol of their remembrance.

Many wept, quietly. Others stood, feeling nothing but the awesomeness of the moment as if time itself had stopped to enclose them all in the stunning fusion of a second borrowed from eternity.

No one but the Reeve noticed that the wreath, which had come to rest against one of the columns of the fallen, left revealed a single name:

EDGAR GEORGE MACINTOSH

* * *

the ceremony was over. It was snowing. Without wind. The flakes descending, their individual shapes intact and uniquely beautiful, tenderly like the exhalation of grace.

* * *

THE DIGNITARIES got into their limousines. No one in the assembly had stirred. No one missed noting the Reeve and his wife flanking His Excellency in the Royal Carriage. They stood — collective in their awe, united in their pride — and watched the entourage as it moved into the snow towards the distant City. They watched until it faded to a blur, shrunk to a solitary dot, and extinguished itself like a black star in the immaculate firmament.

London, Ontario
February 1975 — June 1979

Don Gutteridge lives in London, Ontario, was born in Sarnia and raised in the nearby village of Point Edward. He taught High School English for seven years, later becoming a Professor in the Faculty of Education at Western University, where he is now Professor Emeritus.

He is the author of seventy books: poetry, fiction and scholarly works in educational theory and practice. He has published twenty-two novels, including the twelve-volume Marc Edwards mystery series, and thirty-seven books of poetry, one of which, *Coppermine*, was short-listed for the 1973 Governor-General's Award. In 1970 he won the UWO President's Medal for the best periodical poem of that year, "Death at Quebec."

To listen to interviews with the author, go to:
http://thereandthen.podbean.com.

Fiction:

Bus-Ride. Nairn publishing: Nairn, 1974.
All in Good Time. Black Moss: Windsor, 1980.
St. Vitus Dance. Drumlin: London, 1986.
Shaman's Ground. Drumlin: London, 1988.
How the World Began. Moonstone: Goderich, 1991.
Summer's Idyll. Oberon: Ottawa, 1993.
Winter's Descent. Oberon: Ottawa, 1996.
Bewilderment. Borealis: Ottawa, 2000.
The Perilous Journey of Gavin the Great. Borealis Press: Ottawa, 2010.
The Rebellion Mysteries. Simon and Schuster: Toronto, 2012.
Lily's Story.(e-book). Bev Editions: Toronto, 2013 (Print edition 2014)
Constable Garrett and the Dead Ringer. Tellwell: Victoria, 2016
Lily Fairchild, Tablo publications, 2019.

Marc Edwards Mysteries:

Turncoat. McClelland and Stewart: Toronto, 2003.
Solemn Vows. McClelland and Stewart: Toronto, 2003.
Vital Secrets. Trinity: Saint John, 2007.
Dubious Allegiance. Simon and Schuster: Toronto, 2012.
Bloody Relations. Simon and Schuster: Toronto, 2013.
Death of a Patriot. Simon and Schuster: Toronto, 2014.
The Bishop's Pawn. Bev Editions: Toronto, 2015. (only e-book)
Desperate Acts. Bev Editions: Toronto, 2015. (only e-book)
Unholy Alliance. Bev Editions: Toronto, 2015. (only e-book)
Minor Corruption. Bev Editions: Toronto, 2015. (only e-book)
Governing Passion. Bev Editions: Toronto, 2015. (only e-book)
The Widow's Demise. Bev Editions: Toronto, 2015. (only e-book)

Don Gutteridge has had 37 books of poetry published including his most recent, Hidden Brook Press, books: *Home Ground* – 2018, *Village Dreaming* – 2019, *The Star-Brushed Horizon* – 2019, *Out of the Blue* – 2019, *Inking the World* – 2019, *Rarefied Regions of the Heart: Last Lines* – 2020, followed by his, over 600 page collected works, entitled; *Point Taken* – 2020.